CRAVE

RAI AND SPENCER

A.D. ELLIS

ONE
RAIDEN "RAI" ONO

"YOUR BOY'S HERE, RAI," Chad hollered into the crowded kitchen at Remington's Hometown Diner where I worked as many hours as humanly possible. I was desperately trying to scrape up a down payment for a place of my own. Hell, I didn't even care if it was *all* mine, I just needed to stop sleeping on friends' couches.

I gave my standard grin hoping to keep any attention off me. Chad wasn't a *bad* guy, but he was one of those who toed the line right between *Oh, come on, I'm just having a little fun* and *I'm actually a bully, but I'm so popular and charismatic that no one will ever call me on it.*

"He's not *my boy*," I muttered as I unloaded some dishes onto the shelf. I knew exactly who Chad was talking about. *Spencer Nelson.* Tough guy, perma-scowl, made my heart go all fluttery when I got him to smile or laugh. Definitely not a *boy*. I swallowed thickly as I thought of Spencer's dark hair and eyes, scruffy face, skin that would have likely been pale if not for all of the outside work, and thin-but-strong build.

The first time I'd seen him, I'd been scared to death to wait on him. But I'd quickly learned he only *looked* fierce. In reality, Spencer was soft-spoken, had a great sense of humor, and was pretty easy to talk to once you got to know him.

"Well, whatever you want to call him, he's here." Chad threw an arm around my neck. "He sits in your section—on purpose—every time he comes in. Whether he's ordering a full meal or just coffee, he makes sure to sit at your tables. Even heard him ask for a specific spot one time—*in your section*." Chad had never given me shit about being gay, but I also couldn't tell if he was super comfortable with it or not. "I don't know what kind of spell you've got him under, but the man is all kinds of transfixed. Don't keep him waiting." Chad slapped me on the back. He was built like a damn refrigerator and didn't seem to notice—or care—he was a thousand times stronger than me.

I winced and wiped down the counter. "I'm going. Just needed to do my part here." Taking advantage of the metal side of one of the ovens, I quickly checked my appearance.

My tawny, smooth skin was only slightly flushed from the breakfast rush. I'd long ago gotten over being bored with my plain brown eyes, and there was only so much I could do with my stick-straight inky-black hair.

No way any guy as hot as Spencer would give me a second glance, even if he was gay or bi or pan or whatever. If he was attracted to males, that was only half the battle. Thinking he could be attracted to *me* was laughable.

I was scrawny—okay, maybe not *scrawny*, but I definitely wasn't built or defined the way Spencer was. You could totally tell he got *a lot* of physical exercise. Me? I guess I could thank my Japanese heritage for a thin, lithe build. My parents had always been embarrassed by the fact that I was taller than everyone in our family, but I wasn't *tall* by American standards.

I remembered not knowing how to feel about my height. At home, I was an embarrassment because I was 5'9", which towered over every single family member. At school, I was shorter than almost every single guy in my class.

But feeling torn between school and home was something I'd lived with my entire life. My parents were the first generation of our family to come to America. When they were settled, they brought my grandparents. Over the years, more family members moved from Japan to America. They worked very hard to keep our Japanese roots and traditions alive. And, while I was born in America, I could appreciate being part of two cultures. I loved my heritage.

But I'd also grown up in America and learned a culture that was very different from what my parents and grandparents knew or understood. My family often wasn't okay with my clothes, my choice of friends, my hobbies, the food I ate, or what I chose to study.

At school, I'd kept to a very small group of friends who I had video games and academics in common with. But I was always *too Japanese* for most people at school.

At home, I worked to blend my cultures into something unique that worked for *me*, but my family didn't like that. I wasn't *Japanese enough* for my family.

I solved at least part of that difficult equation when I came out to them right after graduation. I was soon to turn eighteen, I'd graduated with the highest of honors, and I was heading into the medical field.

Sure, my family was disappointed because I'd

chosen *nursing* instead of becoming a doctor, but I figured they'd eventually get over it. I'd done nothing in school without the hope of pleasing my parents and being good enough for them. Looking back on the decision to come out, I should have known anything less than *perfect* in their eyes would have *never* been enough.

A gay son who wanted to be a nurse was more than they could handle.

I'd grown up never wanting for anything and thinking I was loved even if some of the things I did disappointed my family.

With two little words on the night of my high school graduation, I'd found myself homeless, disowned, and poor.

That had happened seven years ago and it still brought me down, but I snapped from the memory as I headed toward Spencer's spot at the breakfast counter. I needed to focus on work and school. Work so I could stay in school and hopefully get a place to stay—I was sooo tired of couch surfing over the past seven years. Sure, I'd found a few more permanent spots from time-to-time, but things would fall through, I'd be short on rent, the owners would move, the list went on and on.

I hadn't been in Remington very long, but I really liked the town. I'd researched carefully to make sure the classes I'd painstakingly taken would transfer to the nearby college before picking Remington as a spot to live. The friend I'd originally moved here to live with had since moved on, but I was determined to make it work. I didn't want to have to pack up and leave another town.

I'd eventually get through nursing school—it was taking a lot longer because I'd had to take extra time to complete my prerequisite courses—and then I could have a nice, permanent, safe place. And Remington was the type of place where I knew I could have that.

But until then, I'd wait on Spencer and count my day as a good one if I got to share a laugh and enjoy his smile. "Hey there, you eating or just coffee?" I asked Spencer.

"Eating. Had a super early job this morning. Gonna eat and nap before heading to another site." Spencer gave me what I was beginning to consider his trademark soft, crooked grin. "Give me the Lumberjack. Scrambled eggs with cheese, bacon and ham, hash browns, waffles, and a big orange juice, please." He flipped up the coffee mug in front of him. "And coffee."

"I don't know how you eat all that and look as good as you do," I said as I scribbled his order. Realizing what I said, I looked at him with wide eyes.

"I mean, you look like you're in good shape, not eating a greasy Lumberjack breakfast two or three times a week." I begged my cheeks to stop burning as I reached behind me for the coffee pot.

"Well, I stay busy. Physical labor is my friend so I can eat like this," Spencer said with a wink as he doctored his coffee with cream and sugar.

I gave a little smile and rushed to the kitchen to put in Spencer's order while I died a thousand small deaths. I was smart, like *super smart* if I was being honest. Why did I always have to sound like such an idiot when I talked to Spencer.

It wasn't like I turned into an idiot around *any* hot guy.

Nope.

Just Spencer.

Okay, that wasn't to say that I was super suave around other hot guys.

I didn't exactly have a lot of hot guys in my life.

I used to hang out with gamer friends and study group friends. But ever since getting kicked out of my home, I pretty much only had the time and energy for work, school, and being friendly enough with classmates and co-workers to bum a couch or floor for as long as they'd have me.

So, I wasn't sure if I'd turn into a bumbling idiot around *any* hot guy or if it was just Spencer. But since I had no one else to test the theory with, I had to assume a lot of my awkwardness had to do with Spencer being Spencer.

I was super busy with a second rush of breakfast customers—which was great for my tips, but meant I didn't get to chat with Spencer much. I was clearly a glutton for punishment because, even though I always made a fool of myself around him, I loved the chance to talk to him.

We exchanged a few pleasantries as I cleared away his meal and gave him his ticket—one day, I hoped to be able to buy a hot guy a meal as a treat. I wasn't there yet, so I just gave a little wave and retreated to the kitchen so I could watch Spencer walk to the counter and pay his bill. He always left a really nice tip—I wasn't dumb enough to think it was just for me, he was probably just a good tipper— and I liked to pretend he liked me for more than just my good customer service.

As was my usual habit, I waited until Spencer headed out the door. Then I made some lame excuse for needing to go to the front and stood for as long as I could next to the door so I could watch him walk to his truck and drive off.

I didn't get to see Spencer every day. And I wasn't desperate enough to *only* have good days when he came in. *But* days I got to see him were always a lot more smiley and floaty. Kinda made it a little easier to forget I was weeks from getting the boot when my current couch situation was no longer viable. Spencer helped me forget that money was always tight, classes didn't pay for themselves, and I was basically alone.

I smiled and bit my lip as I headed to take another order. I knew I didn't have a snowball's chance in hell with a guy like Spencer, but sometimes a little fantasy did the heart a world of good.

TWO
SPENCER NELSON

As TIRED AS I was after a long, exhausting day at a work site, I couldn't help the draw toward the diner. I knew Rai worked mornings and evenings and did classes during the day, so I was very likely to see him if I stopped in—which was something that had quickly become a habit I wasn't even sure I wanted to break. Annnnd, I maybe knew the beat-up little green clunker he drove; if it wasn't there, I'd drive on by.

Bev King, my landlord—kinda more like house mother—and the person I credited for saving me from what could have been a very ugly future, would have dinner ready. I could have easily gone home, taken a shower, and eaten with my found family at Remington Place where I rented a room along with my two best friends and a couple other people.

But just knowing I could spend a little time chatting with Rai before calling an end to my evening was enough to have me mustering a smile and turning my truck into the very sparsely populated parking lot of Remington Hometown Diner.

I didn't fool myself into thinking the bright smile that filled Rai's face when I walked in was for me—at least not *only* for me—but damn, seeing him definitely put a boost in my exhausted steps.

Rai led me to a corner booth way at the back. "We're dead tonight, so I'm covering most of the tables," he explained.

I winced. "Damn, that's a lot."

He waved away my concern. "Nah, we're not at all busy, plus it just means more tips for me."

With a nod, I pushed my luck since he wasn't swamped. "Nursing school, right? Probably pretty expensive."

Rai's melodic laugh had me feeling all floaty. "Definitely. Between trying to pay for my nursing degree one class at a time *and* trying to save up for an apartment, I need all the tips I can get." His face went white. "Shoot, I didn't mean that to sound like I was begging for a tip." He plastered his hand over his face. "I'm so sorry, that sounded horrible."

I laughed—something I didn't do a lot and I had

no clue why I did so much with Rai—and shook my head. "No worries, I didn't take it that way." I glanced at the menu and put in my order in hopes of maybe distracting Rai from his one-sided awkwardness. "I'll have the roast, potatoes, carrots, rolls, and an unsweet tea, please."

Rai flashed me a grateful smile. "Sure thing. I'll get your drink right out."

I scrolled through my phone for a moment, texted Bev to let her know I'd take dinner leftovers for lunch tomorrow, and begged her to leave me some extra dessert if there was any left.

When she replied *It's a good thing I'm not the jealous type or I'd wonder just who has you distracted from our family meals,* I could only crack a wry smile and wonder something very similar. I had no clue *why* I was so drawn to Rai—and it was definitely *Rai*, not the diner—but I wasn't in the mood to analyze it. I liked talking to him. That was enough for me.

"Here you go," Rai said as he brought me a glass of tea. "Food should be up shortly. You lucked out, fresh rolls on their way."

"Nice," I said after taking a sip of tea. I glanced around and saw no one else seated at the tables. "Wow, really is dead, huh?"

Rai laughed. "Yeah. It's past the normal dinner

time, but not late enough for the next round to come in."

"Sit with me," I said and had to fight not to slap my hand over my mouth. When in the hell had I *ever* been the type to invite someone to sit with me?

Rai's cheeks pinked adorably and he slipped into the booth across from me. "For just a minute," he said as he bit his lip.

For just a split second, I wondered what it would be like to take Rai on a date. If I wasn't the lowly construction worker with a fucked-up past and he wasn't my pretty-much-a-complete-stranger-waitperson, we could eat, drink, laugh, and talk. Maybe hit a movie after. Go wander around the mall, play some games at the arcade.

I inwardly rolled my eyes at the thought.

Yeah, right.

Never going to happen.

I'd spent most of my childhood and teen years just trying to survive and my ability to have a relationship or even get involved in *just sex* had been damaged.

I knew I liked guys—which had been hammered home after one *very* awkward encounter with an older woman during high school—but all of my effort had been so focused on just making it through one day at a time, I didn't have the luxury of dating or having a crush or flirting or falling in love.

Which was why the unexplainable pull toward Rai was confusing the hell out of me.

He wasn't the type of guy who usually even caught my eye. Too soft, too fragile, too *smart* that was for damn sure. But I found myself thinking about him constantly, wondering how his day was going, hoping he was safe and comfortable.

I wasn't delusional enough to think that Rai would go for me.

And if by some miracle he *did*, I knew better than to think a guy like Raiden Ono deserved to be strapped with my baggage.

But none of that stopped me from just wanting to be near him, as if just being in his presence could make me better, bring me happiness, wash away the bad shit of the past.

I was lucky I had Bev as a mother figure. When my own mom had finally wasted away thanks to alcohol and drugs—I'd been on my own for some time by that point—I'd been torn between relief and realizing with a pang that I was truly and really all alone in the world.

Finding Bev and Remington Place, having a safe room to rent, becoming friends with Cooper and Dalton—the Scott brothers—and their partners,

Jesse Thompson who owned the place next door and Gabby Harris who worked with Dalton doing some sort of officey shit, was the best thing that had ever happened to me and I was truly grateful.

Being safe, having friends, landing a good job— even if it was as blue collar as construction—put me in a much better place than I'd been most of my life. But even at twenty-eight years old, I knew my past would haunt me forever.

"So, you're looking for a place to live?" I asked without thinking through the question the way I should have. I *knew* there was room at Remington Place. The issue was that the extra spot was in *my* room. I had one of the larger rooms and there was a second bed just waiting for an occupant.

Dre, Bev's nephew, had just moved in to one of the other rooms and he had space too, but since he moved in last he was supposed to be the last to get a roommate.

Cooper was pretty much living full-time next door with Jesse, but he was hesitant to give up his room—almost as if he worried it would jinx whatever he and Jesse had going. Which, by the way, was so sickeningly cute and lovey-dovey I almost puked every time I was around them. But I loved my best friend so I forced myself to be happy for him.

Rai's eyes went wide and he wrinkled his nose.

"Yeah, I'm that guy you see in fictional film portrayals—comes out to his super conservative, traditional family, gets kicked out, and spends seven years barely scraping by, begging for couches or floors to sleep on, and pleading with the universe to cut him some slack." When he stopped talking, his eyes somehow got even wider and he slapped a hand over his mouth. "Shoot, I'm sorry. That wasn't supposed to all come out. I'm twenty-five and you'd think I've never had opportunities for small-talk."

A bell rang and someone hollered, "Order up."

Rai rushed away to get the food.

When he returned, he hovered for a moment.

"If you're busy, it's cool. If not, sit while I eat." I gestured back to the booth with my fork.

Pressing his lips into a thin line as if trying to decide what he *should* do versus what he *wanted* to do, Rai gave a nervous little laugh and slipped back into the pleather booth.

"You looking for a place in Remington?" I asked as I buttered a roll. I offered the second roll to him, but he blushed and shook his head. I got the distinct feeling that he would have gladly accepted the food if not on the clock.

He nodded. "Yeah, keeps me close to work. The college is close and some of my classes and practicums actually take place at Remington Hospital and Medical Center." He shrugged. "I know it's not a huge place, but once I get my degree I can worry about where the best place to work would be. The program I'm in has a really good success rate of graduation and employment."

I took a bite of roast and smirked. "And you're ambitious, I can tell. No way you're not going to be successful."

Rai's cheeks pinked. "You're pretty successful too, I think. Construction, right? What do you build?"

Scoffing, I took a sip of tea before swallowing the bite. "Nothing glamorous. I build and repair houses. Sometimes my crew works on business projects, but usually residential."

"We'd be screwed if no one knew how to build houses," Rai quipped with a tiny shoulder shrug. "You're good at it, I can tell." He cocked his head to the side. "You don't think it's a worthy profession, but you're good at it and you like what you do."

I shrugged, uncomfortable with his level of perception, and shoveled potatoes and carrots into my mouth.

"How did you get into construction?" Rai asked as I chewed.

There was no reason to answer him. I needed to stop coming into the damn diner, needed to stop talking to Rai, needed to wipe him from my mind.

But like the traitor it was, my mouth opened. "I grew up in really unsafe housing. My mom fell through the stairs when I was little. Lost a leg, became an addict, pretty much forgot she had a kid, and I spent the rest of my childhood and teen years dealing with her drunk, high ass, fighting off her abusive boyfriends, and trying to get myself through school."

Rai's hand reached over and squeezed mine.

For a brief moment, the entire world stopped with that one touch.

But he smartened up, yanked his hand away, and mumbled, "I'm so sorry." Whether he was sorry about my mom, my childhood, or holding my hand, I had no idea.

I grunted. "So, I got this crazy idea that if we'd lived in a better house, something built stronger and safer, repaired correctly, things would have been a lot different. That's why construction." I took a long drink. "I can't fix my own shitty past, but I can make sure others have safe housing."

"So, you work only in low-income areas?" Rai leaned in, resting his elbows on the table.

I wiped my mouth and put the napkin back on my lap. "I always take those jobs first, but the crew needs more hours than that so we end up working a variety of jobs."

Rai smiled as if he'd just won a prize. "You're like in charge of the crew or something, right?"

I shrugged. "Yeah, no big deal. Someone had to do it."

He shook his head. "No, you were chosen for that position because you're good at it and you have drive and talent. I can tell." He glanced around the diner as if checking to be sure he could stay with me. "What were you like in high school? I'm betting we wouldn't have been in the same groups."

I laughed. "I was a loner. Always. But I played soccer, tennis, and ran track in hopes of getting some scholarships." The ever-present disappointment of not being good enough washed over me. "Not good enough in sports, not good enough in school, and I couldn't take on loans. I was offered a few need-based scholarships, but by that time, my mom's addiction was *bad* and she started stealing from me. I moved out and never looked back. I had to survive, so that meant getting a job. I lucked out to find a construction company hiring and I worked my way through apprenticeship to where I am now."

Rai cocked his head and studied me. "It sounds as if you feel you let people down by not going to college. But you like your job and you're good at it, why would you feel embarrassed by it?"

I swallowed thickly. "Just seems like it's one more thing where I'll never be enough. I grew up embarrassed of our home, ashamed of my addict mother, knowing I wasn't good enough. I learned quickly that food and shelter were up to me, I couldn't count on my mom, couldn't count on anyone." I stared at my nearly-cleared plate and pursed my lips. "I guess I just feel like I've always been a letdown, not worthy, this guy who could have been so much more. But instead, I just build houses."

Rai shook his head. "I don't see it that way at all. I see someone who was dealt a crap hand who turned around and made the most of what he had. I see a man who pulled himself from a broken, painful past and made something of himself. You have a steady, well-paying job, right?"

I gave a little nod.

"You're good at it. People have strong, safe homes because of you. And whether you want to admit it or not, you enjoy the work. I think you love to work with your hands, love the exhausted feeling after a long, productive day of work." The bell over the door rang to indicate a customer and Rai stood up. "Thanks for letting me chat. You need to cut yourself some slack. If you're happy, that's all that matters."

Rai went to greet the new arrivals. He hadn't said anything that Bev, Cooper, and Dalton hadn't been telling me for over three years, but hearing it from him struck a different chord.

I needed to pay my bill and get out of there before I started wishing for things I couldn't have. Sure, I could make more of an effort in the dating department. I knew Cooper would hook me up if I told him I wanted to get out there—although, I wasn't fully sure that Cooper knew I was gay. But the buzz in my head and thumping in my chest were enough to let me know it wasn't just dating I wanted.

It was Rai.

And that couldn't happen.

Ever.

Rai deserved someone whole, someone who could give him everything I couldn't.

Even as I paid my bill and gave a little wave to Rai, I couldn't help but think that, even if I couldn't get *romantically* involved with him, there was nothing that said I couldn't just be a supportive friend, right?

Was I stupid to think that having Rai in my life as

just a friend would ease that ache I had in my chest whenever I thought about him?

Well, whether it would or not, there was no other option.

It was friendship or nothing.

There was no in-between.

THREE
RAI

I RODE the high of eating dinner with Spencer for a whole two weeks before everything came crashing down. Yeah, yeah, I *knew* I didn't actually eat dinner with him, but he invited me to sit with him so I was counting it as a win.

I'd known the couch I was bumming was going to disappear soon. Suze, a classmate, had been living with her grandmother and offered me the little loveseat in her bedroom—which worked nicely because Suze was hardly ever home so I got her room almost all to myself. But, her grandmother had been slowly worsening in health so she was going to an assisted living home. Suze was moving in with her boyfriend and the house was on the market.

I'd squeaked out a couple extra weeks by offering to keep the place clean for showings and whatnot,

but it all went to shit when the house sold—damn
housing market, just *had* to be efficient, huh? Suze
had called to tell me last night that I needed to
clear out.

Today.

Fudge.

I'd loaded everything I owned—which was
pathetically little—into a couple boxes and shoved
them in my trunk before heading to work.

To make matters worse, my damn piece-of-shit
car decided to crap out on me as I left the diner to
head to class after a fairly crappy morning shift. I
could hoof it, no worries—thank God class was in
Remington for the time being. But, without a place
to stay, my car was going to have to double as my
bedroom for a while and I couldn't very well sleep in
the parking lot of the diner without raising a whole
lotta questions. I had no money to get it towed and
even less than no money to get it repaired.

Fudge.

I'd been grateful to slide into my classes for the
day and gladly took the reprieve they offered. I was
homeless, my car was dead, I needed about five-
hundred more to cover my next school payment, and
I was starving. Which my stomach chose to remind
me of during anatomy and physiology. Normally, I
kept snacks in my car for when I didn't get a chance

to eat properly—or, like now, when I just didn't have the money for food.

But my car was at the diner. Dead as a door knob.

Fudge.

I took a quick break from class to go drink about a gallon from the water fountain in hopes of filling my stomach. I'd have to hope an order got returned that evening and I could sneak some food from the plate. Or maybe Deena, the owner's wife, would toss me the stale crackers when she stocked fresh ones. I'd convinced her I thought they were the best ones. In reality, I just used them to keep myself barely fed.

Thank God for classes.

Academics had always come easy to me and for that I was extremely grateful. There was no way in hell I could have kept up with my degree if the topics were a struggle for me. I was barely scraping by in life the way it was, I couldn't have dealt with classes being stressful on top of everything else.

By the time I left class for the day and rushed back across town in hopes of not being late for my shift, I recognized the beginnings of a breakdown peeking through.

When I first came out and lost my family and home, I'd have breakdowns almost daily. It was massively overwhelming to go from being safe, stable, and pseudo-loved to disowned, homeless, and completely on my own. I'd been scared and hopeless.

As time had gone by and I got jobs, started saving some money, and making a plan, I began to see a light at the end of the tunnel—a damned *long* tunnel, but there was an eventual end—and the breakdowns dwindled to almost nothing. Okay, maybe not *nothing* but very much fewer and farther between.

Over the past seven years, multiple jobs, crazy hours, couch surfing, scrimping and saving every single penny to slowly but surely make something of myself and see my dreams come true had given me a strength and determination I had never known I had. I'd learned how to take things one day at a time while keeping the big prize in mind. I'd learned how to sacrifice. I'd learned how to prioritize.

But days like this, when no matter how hard I worked to hold it together and everything seemed determined to fall apart, there was only so much I could do to fend off a breakdown.

I unlocked my car and scrounged for my box of protein bars.

Empty.

Fudge.

I tossed my backpack on the floorboard and pocketed my keys. No reason to mess with the car right then, it would keep. I needed to get clocked in and hope for amazing tips since I now had to figure out how to get my car towed.

And fixed.

And not miss a payment for school.

And figure out where I was going to live.

At the back door to the diner, where a lot of the workers took their smoke breaks, I paused and took several deep, cleansing breaths.

I have a job. I'm successful in school. Things will get better. Focus on the positives.

I forced myself to smile until it almost felt real and then scurried into the diner in hopes of being so busy I barely had time to breathe, let alone think of all the shit going on in my life.

A few hours later, just when I figured my day really was going to be pure crap because Spencer hadn't come in, the bell over the door rang and a feeling of calm washed over me.

Spencer.

His presence didn't fix any of my issues, but he brought a smile to my face and gave me a little break from the worry.

I didn't get to chat with him much since we luckily were very busy, but I tried to talk as much as possible as I brought him his burger and fries, extra ranch, and a Coke. I drew a smiley face on his bill before sliding it next to his plate. "See ya," I said with a smile. I really didn't have time for more than that, plus I didn't want to seem creeperish if I hovered.

I rushed off to gather my tips and clear tables for people waiting to be seated as Spencer stood to take his bill to the register. After toting the tub of dirty dishes to the back, I emptied the dishes quickly in hopes of getting back to the front to watch Spencer walk to his truck. It was a silly habit—one that probably just made me look desperate—but it was a routine and made me happy.

Trying for nonchalance, which I was never sure I pulled off, I meandered toward the door and glanced out. Spencer's truck wasn't in its usual spot, but a quick scan showed me he was just a few spots down. But no Spencer.

I frowned.

"Looks like your boy hasn't left yet," Chad teased from beside me and I tried not to jump. "You're so creepy the way you watch him walk to his truck every damn time he's here."

"I don't," I started to protest, but there was no reason to argue, so I shrugged instead. "Where is he?" I muttered.

"Who are we looking for?" a voice behind me asked softly.

"Rai has the hots for this construction worker

who comes in all the time," Chad blabbed. "Thinks he's sneaky when he comes up here to watch the guy walk to his truck, but we all know what he's doing."

"Hots for a construction worker?" I heard a smile in the voice.

My chest constricted as my brain registered the familiarity in those words.

Fudge.

My.

Life.

"Yeah, he drives that gray and blue truck. I suppose he's attractive if you're into that type of thing," Chad continued.

"Oh my God, Chad. Can you shut up?" I gritted out.

Chad turned to look at me, confused. When my eyes bugged out of my head, he glanced toward the man behind us. "Oh, hey, it's your boy." Chad laughed. "Found him. Man, can you walk to your truck now so Rai can watch? Put him out of his misery."

The breakdown that had been looming all day crashed down on me and I gave a strangled yeeping noise as I pushed passed Chad and rushed out the back door.

No amount of deep breathing was going to help me avoid the inevitable, but I wanted desperately to escape so I could cry alone. Damn my car for deciding to stop working. I made my way to the far side of the building and settled into a small corner. Tucking my knees up to my chest and praying no one would come looking for me, I buried my face in my knees and cried.

Fudging twenty-five years old and I was crying because of a little stress.

Damn it.

The hot tears burned my cheeks as sobs wracked my body and I hated myself for losing control. But even as the tears fell and I cursed myself, the cathartic relief of a good cry began to seep through me. I despised crying. Despised breaking down—especially in front of others. But I knew it would end with me feeling refreshed, renewed, and ready to tackle my challenges.

I shuddered.

Just had to get all the tears out first. Then I could make a plan.

"Hey, can I sit?" a voice asked and I groaned.

Fudging Spencer.

"I'm fine. You can go," I mumbled.

"I'd rather sit."

Without lifting my head, I gestured vaguely to the spot next to me.

We sat in silence for a few moments. It wasn't

comfortable, but it also wasn't as awkward as I would have expected.

"Rough day?" Spencer asked as he bumped his shoulder against mine.

I snorted into my knees. "Yeah, you could say that."

"Wanna tell me about it? I had a guy staple gun his hand today. Can you beat that?"

I lifted my head, sniffling as I wiped tears from my cheeks. "I'm back to being homeless—I knew it was coming, but I'd been hoping for a little more time. No big, right? I can sleep in my car." I shook my head and ran my hand through my hair. "Except the piece-of-shit decided to crap out on me. Went out to start it before class and it's dead. Can't exactly sleep in my car in the diner parking lot without a lot of questions." I pinched the bridge of my nose, trying without success to stave off a fresh round of tears. "I'm short on my next school payment which means I'll probably have to dip into my down payment money which means I'm taking two steps back from being able to get a place to stay."

My stomach rumbled as it made its presence in the shitastic day known.

"When did you last eat?" Spencer asked.

I waved him off. "Least of my worries. I usually keep protein bars in my car, but the box is empty."

"Can you get a meal inside?" Spencer asked.

"Yeah, but they don't give a discount and it seems wasteful. Once I get paid, I can get a lot more food for ten dollars at the store than one ten-dollar meal."

Spencer shifted and reached into his pocket. "Here, do you have Venmo?"

"I'm not taking your money. No way." God, I was dying.

"Just a loan. Pay me back when you can." He shook his phone at me.

"I get paid in a few days. I'll pay you back. Swear." I told him my Venmo and started planning what I could buy to get the most bang for my buck.

"And I've got an idea if you're down with it," Spencer said warily, almost as if he didn't want to tell me.

I narrowed my eyes. "What kind of plan?"

"Well, I don't know exactly what your housing budget is, but I know for a fact that the place I'm staying is nice and it's *a lot* cheaper than any other place in town." Spencer turned toward me. "Come home with me. See the place. My best friend's boyfriend is a mechanic. I'll help you tow your car to him so he can take a look."

"I don't have the money to pay for a repair right now," I muttered.

"At least let him tell you what's wrong so you'll know what you need to save for. I promise he's good and he's honest; best in town." Spencer stood and reached his hand down to me. "Come on. Even if you don't like the place and don't want the room, you can at least get some food and a good night's sleep. Things will look better in the morning."

I stared at his hand for so long I feared he'd shrug and walk away, taking his offer with him. "Why are you doing this?"

Spencer shrugged. "We're friends. I know what it's like to be at the end of your rope. I understand being on your own and not knowing where to turn; not wanting to be forced into a position where you have to reach out and not being sure you can trust those you're reaching out to."

His words hit hard, like a sucker punch and my heart leaped. Maybe, just maybe, Spencer got it. I reached for his hand and let him pull me to my feet. "Thank you," I whispered.

"Let's leave the car for now. I'll see if Jesse has room for it and then we can get it towed to his shop." Spencer held my hand just long enough for me to notice he was still touching me, but he quickly dropped it and gestured toward the back lot where my car was sitting.

"It's not going anywhere," I answered with a

shrug. "Let me clock out and just grab a few things." I was grateful I was close to the end of my shift and I had my section cleaned and ready for the next shift.

Once I had my belongings and had clocked out, I followed Spencer to his truck. Seeing his blue and gray truck, a fresh wave of embarrassment washed over me. "I'm really sorry for earlier. Being a creeper, all that stuff Chad said, having a meltdown." I curled against the passenger side door as the truck roared to life.

"Don't sweat it," Spencer answered as if he had nerdy little waiters watch him walk to his truck every day. "So, you want to hear about my place?"

"I doubt I can afford the down payment just yet. And I can't do a high monthly payment," I hedged. "But I'd like to hear about it all the same."

"Well, first bit of good news is there's no down payment." Spencer turned my way with a big grin that made his dark eyes sparkle.

"What? Why? How?" I sputtered.

"Well, Bev is the landlord, more like a house mother, and she doesn't charge rent to make money. She owns the house and uses our monthly rent to help with her bill payments some, but mostly to help with upkeep." Spencer turned onto a street named Pleasure Boulevard. A couple blocks down, he took a right onto Remington Way and parked in front of the most gorgeous old Victorian home I'd ever seen. "There she is. 69069 Remington Place at the corner of Pleasure Boulevard and Remington Way," Spencer said with a little sigh.

I gaped, shut my mouth enough to chuckle in disbelief, and then continued to gape. "Holy shit," I whispered. "Not only is she breathtaking, she's also got one of the best addresses I've ever heard of."

Spencer snorted. "Right?"

I shot a look his way. "And you live here? I don't mean to pry, but this place is amazing and huge and...*amazing*," I sputtered. "How do you afford it?"

He smiled softly. "Bev doesn't charge even close to what she should. It's not a money-making situation for her. She always wanted kids, couldn't have any. When her husband died, she thought about making this place into a bed and breakfast type thing, but decided to take in boarders instead. She gets a house full of love and support—and people who adore her and her cooking—and her tenants get a safe, affordable, loving place to stay."

"Will she care that I'm gay?" I asked. Hell, I was pretty sure there was no way I could afford the rent, but I had to make sure I wasn't going to be causing any upheaval.

"Remington Place and Bev don't discriminate. Dalton and his girlfriend live here. Cooper just fell in love with his dad's very male best friend—who happens to be twice his age. Dre...well, I'm not one hundred percent sure on his sexuality, but I'm guessing since he came to live with his aunt after being told he wasn't needed at his parents' that he's got something going on. He'll tell us if and when he's ready." Spencer started to open the door. "Bev doesn't care and no one else here will either."

"And you?" *Please let him be gay. Please.*

But then I realized if he *was* gay, I'd have to deal with knowing he was so far out of my league I'd *never* have a chance.

Okay, no, please let him be straight.

"Gay. But it's not something I've spent a lot of time embracing or getting to know." Spencer's eyes traveled up and down my body and he swallowed. "I don't do the dating or relationship thing."

I cocked my head to the side and frowned. "Really? Why? I figured you'd be batting them off with a stick."

He shrugged. "Never had time. Surviving took precedence. Now, I'm just not sure how to make it work."

"So, you're a virgin like me?" *Holy fudging shit, Rai. You moron! You just announced to the hottest guy in the world that you're a twenty-five-year-old virgin. Fuuuudge.* My face flamed hot enough to rival molten lava. "Oh my God," I whispered as I buried my head in my hand. "Can we just forget everything I said in the last sixty seconds?"

Spencer's face was twisted up in what appeared to be pain, but he just nodded and made some sort of grunting sound. "Yeah, no worries."

I scurried from the truck and stood on the sidewalk staring up at the gigantic, gorgeous house. "I can't believe this place is even real. *No way* could I ever get lucky enough to live here."

Spencer stood beside me and cleared his throat. "I'll introduce you to Bev and get you something the eat. Then I'll show you around. If you're interested, I'll let Bev talk to you about rent and whatnot."

I nodded. The stress of the day was catching up to me—probably the hunger, too—and a wave of exhaustion fought valiantly to overtake my growing excitement.

"Bev, I wanted to introduce you to someone," Spencer said as we walked into the kitchen. "This is my friend Raiden Ono. Rai, this is my Bev."

My Bev. How dang sweet was that? More proof that Spencer's gruff appearance and perma-scowl didn't match his heart.

An older woman—I immediately wanted to hug her and call her Grandma, but I refrained—turned from the stove with a kind smile as she wiped her hands on her apron. Her dark skin was flushed, likely from whatever was cooking and smelling so delicious, but her kind eyes sparkled as she took me in. "Welcome to Remington Place. I'm Bev King. We'll get you settled in after dinner. I need to get some food in you before you fall right over."

Spencer chuckled as I was pulled into one of the best hugs I'd ever received—I was helpless to stop it, even if I'd wanted to.

"Oh, um, I'm not sure I can stay," I sputtered as Bev patted my cheek and turned back to the stove, her day dress swirling around her short, ample legs.

"Nonsense, we'll talk after dinner." Bev took a dish from the oven. "Spence, go ahead and introduce him. Save the detailed tour for after we eat."

Understanding quickly that you didn't argue with Bev, I scurried to follow Spencer from the kitchen. "She's amazing. Scary, but amazing."

Spencer laughed. "She *can* be scary, but mostly it's all done out of love. She's super smart, strong, and doesn't play games." He elbowed me gently. "She likes you."

"What? How can you tell?"

"Well, she knows anyone any of us brings home are good people, but I could see it in her eyes. She likes you; don't go thinking you'll take my place as favorite though," Spencer teased.

"Favorite? Riiiight," a super cute guy about my age, messy bleach blond hair, gray eyes, and pale skin bounded from the couch where he and a little girl had been reading a book.

"This is my friend, Rai Ono," Spencer said.

"Hi, I'm Cooper Scott. This is Hadley and her dad, Jesse Thompson." A very attractive man, definitely older than Cooper, stood from a recliner and shook my hand.

Hadley smiled shyly. "Cooper is my daddy. That's really my grandpa," she pointed to Jesse, "but I call him Dad because my mom died."

I blinked as the information soaked in. Wow, definitely not a traditional family, but they seemed happy and well-adjusted—Hadley most of all. "It's nice to meet all of you."

"Save the best for last, huh? Good plan," a man and woman walked into the room. "Hi, I'm Dalton Scott, Cooper's older brother." There was a resemblance between the men, but I wouldn't have immediately pinned them as brothers.

"I'm Gabby Harris, Dalton's better half," said a petite woman with huge brown eyes behind trendy glasses and a head full of some of the most gorgeous spiral curls I'd ever seen. The teal eyeshadow she wore popped on her soft, brown skin and her smile lit up the room.

"Best for last? You know that's right," a gorgeous man with long braids pulled back from his face and a broad smile came into the room. "I'm Andre King, Bev's nephew and house favorite," he teased. "Call me Dre."

"I'm Rai. It's great to meet all of you," I said, doing my best not to stammer. I wasn't the type who didn't like people, but meeting all of them at once had been a bit overwhelming.

"So, you're taking the bed in..." Cooper started, but Spencer cut him off.

"Bev said it's time to eat," Spencer said and steered me back toward the kitchen before Cooper could finish his sentence.

Throughout the meal, I tried to keep up with the chatter, but I found myself lost and just enjoying the delicious food. I caught Cooper glancing at me a couple times with a curious smile on his face, almost as if he was trying to figure me out, but I wasn't sure what—if anything—to read into it.

About halfway through dinner, Cooper's eyes widened and he smiled broadly as he tapped his fingers on the table. "I *knew* I recognized you from somewhere!" he crowed. "The diner, right? You work at the diner?"

Spencer stiffened next to me, but I didn't see any

reason to lie about where I worked. "Yeah, I work there."

Cooper just smiled, gave Spencer a look, and elbowed Jesse in some silent communication before the whole crew returned to eating.

The meal of baked chicken, roasted potatoes, asparagus, green beans, macaroni and cheese, and thick-sliced, buttered bread was probably the best I'd ever eaten and I had to force myself to eat slowly so as not to get a stomachache.

"Too full or save room for dessert?" Bev asked as we all worked to clear our plates from the table a bit later.

"I'm so damn full, but I know that's chocolate lava cake and it's best hot so I'm going to have to have a piece before we leave," Jesse said with a groan.

Everyone opted into dessert despite being full from the delicious meal.

I moaned as I took a bite of the warm, gooey cake. Seriously, no dessert in the history of desserts would ever compare.

Spencer shot me a look I couldn't decipher, but he quickly covered it with a smile. "Told you Bev's the best cook ever."

I savored another bite. "Why in the world would you waste your time eating at the diner when you have *this* waiting for you at home," I wondered aloud.

Cooper and Dalton snorted and turned toward Spencer as if ready to pounce.

"Mmhm, just the question I've been wondering," Bev said sweetly. "Now," she gave a pointed look to the brothers which had them backing off whatever teasing they'd been preparing to do, "it's time for Spencer to show Rai around while I finish in here. Then you and I," she gave me a kind smile, "we'll talk business."

Spencer stood and gathered several things from the table and the rest of us followed suit. It seemed as if Bev didn't expect help in the kitchen, but the crew of Remington Place pitched in anyway because it was the right thing to do. I liked that.

"Come on," Spencer said when the only thing left for Bev to do was rinse a few dishes. "I'll show you around."

My eyes struggled to take in all of the beauty as Spencer walked me through the house. The intricate original designs in the dark wood, the gorgeous staircase, just the *history* in the place was astounding. Kitchen, bathroom, Bev's room, living room, dining room, sitting room, office, and a fantastic little nook took up the ground floor.

"We'll start on the very top floor," Spencer said as he led me up the grand staircase. Once on the second floor, he walked me to a much smaller staircase and we found ourselves on the third floor which housed only a bathroom—which had been an addition to the house —and two bedrooms. Dalton and Gabby had one of the rooms while Dre was in the second. There was an empty bed in Dre's room and I wondered if that was where I'd be staying. "Dre was the last person to move in. Bev usually goes by the rule that the last to move in is the last to get a roommate," Spencer explained.

"Ah, makes sense," I said as I followed him down to the second floor. The space was slightly bigger with a bathroom—again, an addition, but larger than the third-floor bathroom—two bedrooms, and a foyer area that looked as if it was used for video games.

"That's Cooper's room," Spencer said as he pointed to the smallest of all the rooms we'd seen so far. "His is the smallest, so it's been just a single. But I think two could fit if needed."

I glanced at the room. "Yeah, would be tight, but it would work. Does he not stay here?"

Spencer rubbed the back of his neck. "Well, he's pretty much moved in with Jesse—he lives next door —but Cooper worries about giving up his space here permanently. I think he kinda worries it will jinx what he and Jesse have going on."

I nodded. "Giving up a place to stay when you're not guaranteed of another is difficult. I get it." I cleared my throat. "Not to be nosy, but Hadley called Cooper Daddy..." I trailed off, not sure how to continue my question.

"Jesse is Hadley's grandfather. His estranged wife, Nicole, and their daughter, Lauren, were killed by a drunk driver around six years ago. Jesse moved here a little over a year ago; Cooper became his nanny." Spencer smirked. "And the rest, as they say, is history."

"They seem really happy."

He nodded. "They are. Cooper was so damn happy the day Hadley said she wanted to call him her daddy. They aren't living a *perfect* life, but pretty close to it."

"Perfection isn't needed. It shouldn't be our goal. Our goal should be to find beauty and happiness in the imperfect," I said as I turned from Cooper's smaller room and slammed my elbow into the doorframe. "Fuuuudge," I groaned as I rubbed the injury.

Spencer smiled softly as he took my elbow and rubbed it. "*Fudge?* You don't cuss?"

Elbow still throbbing, but my hot cheeks taking

over the attention, I shrugged. "I cuss. But the F word was something my parents and grandparents abhorred. I grew up thinking it was the worst of the worst." I wrinkled my nose. "Silly, I know, because I'll say pretty much any other cuss word, but I can't bring myself to say that one." I glanced at the floor. "One more thing that makes me nerdy and different."

He shook his head. "Nah, I like it. It makes you unique; it's never bad to have something you stand for."

I scoffed. "I think I'd be better off standing for something that *helps* others, not just unable to utter a damn swear word all because it makes me feel like my family will hear me and curse me from here to damnation."

Spencer chuckled. "Do you *want* to use the word? If it's needing practice with it, I can help."

"Not really. I know I look young and probably seem like a baby compared to you, but I've made it a quarter of a century without needing to say it, I think I'm good." I shoved my hands in my pockets.

An evil grin filled Spencer's face and he moved closer. "What about when you're all hot and heavy with a guy and you want to take things further? You gonna tell him you want him to fudge you?"

A laugh bubbled from me, mixed with extreme

embarrassment, but I couldn't help it, I liked Spencer's teasing. I pursed my lips. "I don't know, I guess I'd never thought about it. What are my other options?" I scowled.

"Screw me? Do me?" Spencer's shoulders shook. "The tried-and-true *make love to me?*" Something flashed in his eyes before he looked away.

"Ugh, I don't know. None of them sound like they'd make a guy want to do anything with me," my mouth twisted around the words.

Spencer cleared his throat. "Pretty sure that won't be a problem." He gestured across the foyer to a closed door. "So, um, there's a bit of a detail I kinda haven't told you yet. Wanted you to see the place, meet the people, eat the food—honestly, I was trying to win you over before I had to tell you."

Off-kilter from the sex conversation, even if Spencer had just been teasing, I could only scowl as I waited for whatever Spencer had to say. I took slow breaths trying to calm my anxiety.

"The open bed is in here," he said as he swung open the door to one of the biggest rooms we'd seen.

I glanced around the area and gulped. *Oh hell, no. How could I be so lucky? Or maybe it was unlucky? Fuuudge.* "Is this..."

Spencer grimaced. "You'd be rooming with me. I know it's not the best situation and I'd fix it if I could, but it's the option for now. I'm sorry it's all I can offer."

I blinked rapidly for several seconds.

Sharing a room. That wasn't a problem when I was used to making do with whatever couch or floor I could find.

Sharing a room with Spencer?

Fudge.

Spencer.

The hottest guy I'd ever met.

Spencer.

The guy so far out of my league we weren't even on the same planet.

Spencer.

The friend who understood what I was going through and offered me a place to stay even if it meant giving up half of his room.

"It's a warm bed in a safe, loving home. You could tell me I had to room with an ogre and I'd still feel grateful for a place to sleep." I offered Spencer a smile that I hoped let him know I was completely okay with being his roommate while *not* showing him how desperately I wanted my fantasy world to come to life so he'd see me as someone other than a nerdy, down-on-his-luck friend.

"You got something against ogres?" Spencer joked.

"As long as I don't have to sleep in my car, I'll deal."

"Well, I promise I shower and keep my side of the room neat. Can't guarantee it, but I don't *think* I snore." Spencer gestured toward the stairs while I laughed. "You can talk with Bev and get the money stuff figured out. I'll go check with Jesse about the car."

Wanting to argue about the car being *my* responsibility, but recognizing that it was pointless, I let Spencer go while I went to the little sitting room where Bev was kicked back with what appeared to be a mug of tea. She had a notebook and a pen in her lap and she smiled when she saw me. "Come in, come in. Let's get these details ironed out. You look like you're about ready to drop."

Smiling gratefully and sinking onto the comfy couch, I said, "It's been a really long day."

"Long day? Or a bit more than that?" Bev asked, a knowing look on her face.

I sighed. "Seven years." After that admission, my entire story came pouring out. It wasn't that I normally *hid* my past, I just wasn't in the habit of blabbing it to everyone I met. And now I'd shared it with both Spencer and Bev.

She listened and nodded, not interrupting, just letting me spew the words.

"I'm not trying to get pity or anything. I'm pretty sure I won't be able to afford a place as grand as this, but I'd love to hear the price for future reference if I ever save up enough." I worked hard to keep my heavy eyes from fluttering asleep while preparing for the disappointment I knew was coming. "And I appreciate the meal more than you know. Hadn't been that hungry for a while and it made me realize how good I've usually got it."

"I like that you can see your blessings even in the midst of turmoil; that's a good trait to have." Bev opened her notebook and made some notes before flipping through a few pages. "Well, you're in luck that Spencer has his half of the room open. Dre would have been my second choice for you, but I'd like to give him a bit more time to settle in—I'm probably biased with him being my nephew and all, but I want him to really get snug in his place here so he doesn't bolt." She waved a hand as if dismissing her thoughts. "But that's neither here nor there." Bev made a few marks on the paper and clicked her tongue. "Well, I wish I could offer you something a little lower," she began and my heart sunk.

I'd *known* better than to let myself get too excited about the prospect of living at Remington Place.

"Three hundred a month is the lowest I can go right now. If we take in another tenant or two, I can maybe shave off a bit." Bev closed her notebook and looked at me expectantly.

My mouth fell open. "Three hundred? *A month?* Are you crazy? A room in a place like this anywhere else would easily be close to a grand a month." My throat was dry as I tried to swallow. "Three hundred a month would *maybe* get me a room the size of your bathroom, moldy, dirty, and falling apart. In a very unsafe part of town." I held my head in my hands. "You can't be serious." I glanced up at Bev. "You're not serious, are you? This is like a joke?"

She smiled softly. "No joke. Three hundred a month. First day or last day, I don't mind as long as it's paid. And if payment one month becomes an issue, come talk to me." She opened the notebook again and made a note. "You're welcome to buy your own groceries if you'd like something I don't keep on hand, but the groceries I buy are for the whole house. I cook what I want to cook, but I make meals with everyone in mind. I do ask for help with keeping the place clean and tidy. If there are repairs that need done or special projects, I'll ask for help."

I couldn't stop nodding in a daze.

"No drugs. I don't mind if you drink, but moderation is the key. You can bring people home, but be respectful of your housemates. Communication is a must; if there's an issue, we talk it out." Bev tossed her notebook aside. "So, what do you say? Are you making Remington Place your home?"

Tears burned my eyes and I couldn't help the little bubble of laughter that escaped. "Yeah. Definitely. Thank you so much." I stood just as she did and threw my arms around her. "Thank you. This is...it's just too much...like I'm going to wake up and realize it's just a dream."

"No dream," Bev said as she rubbed my back. "We're glad to have you as part of our family. Now, before you fall asleep standing up, you head on upstairs. Spencer texted that he and Jesse went to pull your car to the shop. Take a shower. I'll toss some spare clothes on the bed until you get your belongings here."

Thirty minutes later, dressed in someone else's clothes, I stood in *my room* looking at *my bed* and the entire day—hell, the entire seven years—came crashing down on me as tears poured and sobs wracked my body.

FOUR

SPENCER

"Easy as that?" I asked Jesse as he slammed the hood closed on Rai's clunker.

"Yep, loose battery cable. I cleaned up all the corrosion and tightened everything up. Should be good as new." Jesse wiped his hands on a rag.

"How much do I owe you?"

Jesse raised a brow. "How much do *you* owe me for *Rai's* car?"

I lifted a shoulder. "He's in a bit of a situation. Thought I'd help him out."

Jesse studied me for a moment then nodded. "No charge."

"Really? I can pay."

"Nah, really. Maybe would have charged a customer twenty-five, tops—and probably not even that—but not charging a friend for something that took less than twenty minutes." Jesse tossed the rag in a bucket and grabbed a beer and a water from the shop fridge. Tossing me the water, he gestured toward the little patio.

I appreciated that no one ever questioned why I didn't drink, never tried to goad me into it. I'd watched my mother drink and drug herself to death, I had no desire to do the same. Maybe it was the memories of how badly she stank of alcohol— whether on her stained clothes, her sweat-drenched body, or the vomit I used to have to clean up—but I couldn't even bring myself to smell hard liquor, let alone swallow it down. And beer wasn't much better, so I stuck to water, tea, and soda.

We settled at the table and both took long swigs from our bottles.

"Thanks a lot for your help tonight. I know Rai is going to be so relieved that the issue was an easy one to fix."

"Oh, hey," Cooper said as he came to join us, "got one of those for me?" He rubbed Jesse's back as he walked to the shop to grab his own beer before joining us. "She's asleep. Only took three stories."

I laughed. I knew that Hadley was the queen of *one more story* at bedtime. The kid had even roped me into reading to her when she spent the night at Bev's.

"Soooo," Cooper drawled and gave me a shit-eating grin.

"What?" I deadpanned.

"Cutie from the diner is now your roomie? That has potentially disastrous slash possibly incredible written *all* over it," Cooper said as he attempted to look innocent.

"It has absolutely *nothing* written on it. Nowhere, no how. Can't happen. Not gonna happen. End of story, so don't go getting your little romantic brain all in a tizzy."

Jesse chuckled and took Cooper's hand.

"I'm *just saying…*"

"Well, *stop,*" I interrupted.

Of course, he didn't. "The way you two look at each other is sizzling hot."

"How do you even know I'm gay?" I challenged.

Cooper opened his mouth, closed it, cocked his head to study me, then smiled with a shrug. "I don't know. It's never been something we've talked about, never been a thing, but there's something about the way you look at him that just gives it away." He took a long drink of his beer. "Am I wrong? You're at least bi, right? You think he's hot."

I growled and swallowed some water. "And just how do I look at him?" I grumbled.

"Like you want to wrap him up and protect him

right before you lick him up one side and down the other with all kinds of sexy stops in between."

I groaned, trying to make it sound like Cooper was being ridiculous, but mostly because the picture he painted was one I did *not* need in my head. Choosing to ignore the mental imagery Coop was spewing, I rolled my eyes. "You're not wrong, I *am* gay. But whether I find Rai attractive or not plays no part in me inviting him to live here. He needed a place."

Cooper held up a hand. "Oh no, I'd never think you brought him here for anything other than a place to stay. In fact, I'm pretty sure it almost killed you to have to offer because you *knew* it would put him in your room—but you're too good of a person to leave him struggling."

I nodded, glad that Cooper got that.

"I'm just saying that you two look at each other like you want to eat the other one up, you're single— I was going on the assumption Rai was single if he didn't have a boyfriend willing to help him out— what's the harm in having a little fun?" Cooper held up the hand still firmly grasped in Jesse's. "Look where our little bit of fun got us."

"Whole lotta different here," I groused. "Plus, I don't do relationships or dating or any of that shit." Our love lives weren't things we'd talked about much in the past—at least not *mine*—and I would have preferred to keep it that way.

Cooper cocked his head. "Why?"

"I don't really know how. You know how fucked up my childhood was. Didn't learn about solid, loving relationships. Didn't have time for crushing or flirting or dating when I was trying to get through one day at a time." I shrugged. "Easier to just avoid."

Cooper shook his head, his mouth drawn down. "That's sad."

I shot him a look that clearly said I didn't want his pity.

"So, you only do hook-ups?" he asked, changing tactics.

"If that," I rolled my shoulders. "Porn and my right hand work fine."

"So, you're a virgin?" Cooper's eyes went wide.

"No," I spat. "But Rai is, so don't make it out like it's a terrible thing." I finished my water. "I've had sex. Decent sex. *Really* bad sex. But none of it with people I actually liked or wanted to see again."

The thought of Rai being a virgin was likely going to drive me insane. Either because I wanted him so badly and wanted what no one else had ever had *or* because I'd make myself crazy thinking about the fact some other guy was going to get to kiss him, touch him, fuck him. Or *fudge him* I thought with a snort.

Cooper and Jesse both gave me weird looks, but I just shrugged them away.

"How old is Rai?" Jesse asked after a moment.

"Twenty-five," I answered. When they both looked shocked, I nodded. "I know. He looks a lot younger. And I think the trauma of losing his family and being kicked out on his own has kinda made him seem even younger—maybe like he sort of froze in time as that eighteen-year-old? He's hella smart and responsible and mature beyond his years in some ways, but in others, he seems a little...stunted? He thinks of himself as an awkward nerd, I just think he's not had a lot of experience with close, supportive friends and family." Which was *exactly* why he needed Bev and Remington Place.

Cooper pursed his lips. "I won't bug you about it," he began and shot us both looks when Jesse and I snorted. "I'm just saying that you two are definitely attracted to each other. You've got the proximity, you're both single, I guess I don't see what the harm would be."

"The harm," I growled, "would be putting someone as good and kind, with such amazing potential, in a situation with someone like me."

"Someone like you?" Cooper made a face.

"Successful? Kind-hearted and caring? A talented, hard worker?"

I huffed and rolled my eyes. "Try seeing me from a lens *other* than my best friend. I'm nothing more than a blue-collar worker with a fucked-up past and an inability to love."

Jesse cleared his throat. "Nothing wrong with a blue-collar job. You provide safe homes and you're very talented. Speaking as a fellow *blue* and someone with baggage galore, don't let that be what keeps you from finding happiness."

I shook my head. "No offense meant."

Jesse waved it off.

"I've known I was worthless since my very first memories. I don't *want* a relationship—they only end in heartache—and I don't deserve one of the good ones." I stood up. "Rai is a great guy. I like him. He's *my friend.*"

"And when he wants more than that?" Cooper asked softly.

"He won't," I argued. "He'll find someone worth his time, someone who deserves every good thing about him." I tossed my empty bottle in the recycling tub. "Thanks again for your help, Jess. See ya guys tomorrow probably."

I walked toward Remington Place, my head and heart a jumble of thoughts. There was no way Rai and I could be anything more than friends. No way Rai would even want anything more than friends. That didn't change the fact that I found myself wildly attracted to him, but that was a fact I'd have to keep to myself and *never* act on. Rai Ono was my friend and only my friend. Anything else I wanted him to be would just have to live in my imagination.

That way, when he fell in love and moved on, I could lock it all away, act as if it never happened, and not even miss a beat.

But it didn't mean I wouldn't be dreaming about him.

No, it didn't mean *that* at all.

I checked in on Bev when I got to the house. "You and Rai work things out?"

She nodded as she stirred a mug of warm milk—her favorite treat at bedtime. "We did indeed. I gave him the lowest I could go for now; seems that rent has gone down a bit recently," she said with a wink. "Delighted to have him here, seems like a real gem. He's lucky to have you."

"He doesn't *have* me," I said, much too quickly.

Bev narrowed her eyes at me and pursed her lips. "As a friend?"

Shit.

"Oh, yeah. Of course, as a friend. That goes without saying," I stammered.

She cocked her head. "Mmhm," she hummed. "Well, if I survived Cooper and Jesse, I'm sure I can survive whatever you and Raiden might bring my way."

I ran a hand over my face. "We're not bringing you *anything*. He's a friend. Nothing more."

She continued to study me. "You're not attracted to him? Because I thought I caught a vibe..." she trailed off to sip her warm milk.

I huffed. "Yes, fine. I'm attracted to him." Like crazy attracted to him. "But he deserves better than me."

Bev wagged a finger my way. "Don't you dare. You are a special person and the right man will be *lucky* to earn your love." She held her mug between both hands as if to absorb the warmth. "What if Raiden chooses you? Isn't it his place to decide what he *deserves*?"

"First, he won't," I insisted. There was no way a guy like Rai was going to go for a guy like me. We were too different. I crossed my arms over my chest. "And second, I'll take the high road and let him down easy. I'll be his friend, I'll support him, keep him safe, and all that. Hell, I'd be willing to keep it *just sex* if that's what he wanted—makes it a little rough being roommates—but sex or friendship or both is all I'll do. A serious relationship? Possibility of *love*? They sound great in theory, but I'm not made for that. Even if it was something I desperately wanted, I can't—*won't*—saddle him with a damaged heart and mediocre future." I leaned in to kiss Bev's cheek before her sad eyes could make me feel any worse.

"My wish for you is that you'll finally recognize your worth. Your heart is huge and so willing to give." Bev placed a hand on my arm. "I want *you* to love *you*. And I want you to find a person who deserves what you have to offer and gives it right back to you."

"Wishes don't come true," I muttered. Believe me, if they did, I wouldn't have had such a shitty childhood.

Bev smiled sadly and walked toward her room, but she stopped and turned back to me. "Sometimes, the wishes we're making just aren't meant to be or they come to us looking different than what *we* think we want or need. I wished and wished until I could wish no more for children of my own. That specific wish never came to be, but look at what I have now. A house full of my children, surrounded by love. It wasn't the way I dreamed it, but it's exactly what I needed." She tilted her head to the side. "And I think maybe it's the way some of my babies needed it to work out, too." She gave a little nod. "Good night. Love you."

I swallowed thickly. "Love you." I watched her walk to her room before I started up the stairs. Where would I be without Bev? If all of her wishes and dreams for children of her own had come true, would she have bought the house and opened Remington Place to boarders? Would I have met Cooper and Dalton? I didn't like the thought that Bev had to suffer her wishes not coming true just so *I* could end up with a safe place to stay. But selfishly, I also couldn't regret it. Bev and this place had saved me.

Bev's wish for me was sweet and heartfelt. But I'd spent most of my life knowing that Spencer Nelson didn't get the happy ending, didn't get support, didn't get the love everyone spouted on about.

But you're surrounded by love and support here.

I shook my head and gritted my teeth. That was different. That was just for now—I knew the other shoe would drop, it always did. In the grand scheme of things, I was on my own—*I* was the only one I could count on—and I knew what my future held. The years ahead of me weren't dismal, no, I'd have a job I enjoyed and be able to support myself. But *Rai's* future was bright—and he didn't deserve me dulling that shine. If he wanted me there as a friend, I'd be there in a heartbeat.

While hiding your true feelings like a coward.

I pushed the thought away and smiled as I recognized the scent of body wash. Rai had showered and was likely asleep. I'd give him the good news about his car in the morning.

When I opened the door to my room—*our* room —it took a moment for my eyes to adjust to the darkness, but I immediately sensed Rai wasn't in his bed. I glanced toward the window and saw him at the exact moment I heard his sob.

"Hey, you okay?" I asked, stepping closer.

Rai turned with a quiet sniffle and launched himself into my arms. With no time to think, I simply wrapped him up and held him as he cried. He shivered as my hand traveled up and down his back. "I'm sorry, everything just kinda washed over me at once. I'm going to stay, Bev's letting me pay a ridiculously low amount a month—like *insanely* low, but she insists it's what she wants. I can't even imagine being able to pay for classes, hell, maybe I can even take more at one time. Plus having money for food and gas. Maybe even being able to go out some." He shook his head against my chest. "Thank you so much for bringing me here. I know it sucks to have to share your room, but you seriously saved me." Rai's eyes gleamed in the moonlight as he looked up at me. When he leaned in, I held my breath and savored the touch of his lips against my cheek. "Thank you," he whispered.

"You're welcome, but don't think that I'm upset to have you here. You're a friend and I'm glad we could work it out." The more I drove home the *friend* part, the better. I didn't *think* Rai had a crush on me, but if Cooper and Bev were to be believed, it was best for me to squash it now. And keep reminding myself of the same.

"It's been so long since I've had *my own* bed to sleep in. I may crawl in and never be able to get out," Rai murmured, still wrapped in my arms. Still way too close, smelling way too good. "Oh! My car. How bad is it?" he grimaced as if preparing for bad news.

Taking the opening to break the seriousness, I let him go and walked to put the contents of my pockets onto my dresser. "Good news. Jesse said it was just a loose battery cable. He did some work on the corrosion and tightened things up, said you should be good to go."

Rai's eyes went wide and a fresh wave of tears started. "For real? What do I owe him? Sounds like maybe it won't cost an arm and a leg."

"He said nothing. Said he likely wouldn't even have charged a customer and he definitely wasn't charging a friend." I shrugged and grabbed some clothes. Getting used to having someone else in the room was going to take some time. No more walking around in my underwear or less.

Rai flopped down on his bed and smiled through his tears. "If this is a dream, please don't wake me up. Just let me enjoy it for a little while longer."

I chuckled and headed toward the door to grab a shower.

"Even during the worst of my struggles, I never took for granted that I was still privileged compared to so many in the world. No one should ever have to know hunger or think of a damn bed as a luxury," he murmured sleepily. "I think maybe someday, I want to work with a program that helps those less fortunate. Medical services, food, basic shelter, and clothing; I never want to take my place in this world for granted. You've given me a chance to start over and live my dreams; I want to pass it on someday." His words were slurred and I thought he likely fell asleep before the last syllable was muttered.

But I stood at the door watching him and thinking about his words. Yeah, Rai was going to go on to do amazing things. The world deserved his greatness and he deserved every good thing fate wanted to pile onto him. Without thinking, I walked to his bed and spread a blanket over him, tucking it under his chin, and gritting my teeth when he hummed and curled onto his side.

How badly do you want to crawl into that bed and hold him close?

I backed away from Rai's bed as quickly as I could and escaped to the bathroom. Didn't matter how badly I wanted that, it couldn't happen. Rai needed to be permanently friend-zoned.

Talk about a mind-fuck when ten minutes later, that *friend* starred in my shower jack-off session. With a final spurt of cum against the shower wall, I groaned as guilt washed over me, my balls still tingling and my dick spent, images of Rai heavy in my mind. In real life, he'd be in the friend-zone. In my head, all was fair game.

I was only human after all.

FIVE

RAI

IT WAS AMAZING what having a stable, safe place to stay could do for a person's psyche. I'd been at Remington Place for over a month and had truly never been happier. Knowing where my next meal would come from and getting a good night's sleep were truly life-changers.

I was still working at the diner, but I wasn't working every waking hour. I'd paid my school payment and put aside enough for the next one, plus, I was going to take an additional class next semester. I was slowly setting aside money for future months' rent; just having the ability to get ahead felt so damn good.

After talking to Jesse about my car's tire situation, I was saving a bit from each paycheck to save up for four new tires; not top-of-the-line ones, but tires that actually had some tread.

I'd even started going to a local game shop and playing in some of their groups.

And...

I'd fallen *hard* for Spencer.

Yeah, before I moved into his room, I'd thought he was hot and I loved chatting with him. After a month of living with him? Seeing him every damn day—sleep-lined face, bed head, sleeping in just his boxers, yanking on his work jeans, stretched out on his bed while he scrolled through his phone? All of those things—plus about a million more tiny details I'd learned about him—plus the fact that we got to laugh and joke and just spend time together as friends rather than customer and waiter had me moving from an easy crush to a full-on head-over-heels obsession with the man.

And there was absolutely nothing I could do about it because Spencer had clearly friend-zoned me. I got it, I really did. No way someone as hot as Spencer would go for a nerdy guy like me. I knew I *looked* and maybe came across younger than I really was; my life experiences had forced me to grow up way too fast in some ways and stunted my social growth in others.

But despite how ridiculous it was, I couldn't help

but pine for Spencer and wish something would change between us. I liked him—*a lot*—and I didn't want to give up being friends with him, but I wanted more.

Before I moved into Remington Place, I didn't really have much time to think about crushes or dating, I was too worried about making sure I had the basic necessities and my next class payment.

With the extreme weight of all of those things off my shoulders, I was able to give time and attention to other things.

Aside from enjoying the gaming group with some people I could definitely see becoming friends—there was one new guy, who also happened to be in some of my classes, who unfortunately and aggressively seemed interested in more than friendship—I now had all the time in the world to focus on how badly I wanted to be with Spencer.

And how badly he *didn't* want me.

Cooper had suggested that perhaps that wasn't true when we played video games one day.

"So, you and Spencer seem to be working out well, huh?" Cooper had asked.

I'd sighed. "Yeah, I guess."

Cooper had smiled. "You two are too cute. When are you just going to admit you like each other?"

My eyes had grown wide and I'd started to protest,

but I knew I could trust Cooper so I'd flopped backward against the couch and groaned. "I like him so much and I'd totally admit to it if I thought it would change anything between us. But he doesn't see me that way."

Cooper had cocked a brow. "I wouldn't be so sure about that. Spencer doesn't really know how to do the whole relationship thing. I don't think it's so much about him not liking you as it is about him not knowing how to like and accept himself."

I'd huffed. "Well, how in the world do I get him to see me as more than just a friend he needs to protect?"

Cooper was quiet for a moment. "I think he'll have to be in a situation where he has no choice but to realize he likes you and he can't avoid it no matter how hard he tries." He'd shaken his head. "I don't have the perfect answer, but I think you guys will probably get there eventually. I mean, the attraction sizzling between you two is off the charts. Can't imagine either of you will be able to ignore that for much longer."

Which was how I'd come to a monumental, likely very terrible, decision. I had a plan. It involved Lance, the guy in the gaming group and some of my classes who seemed to want more with me, and me asking Spencer for his help.

My plan was two-fold. One, it would hopefully get Lance to back off. Two, it would give me a reason to get up-close and personal with Spencer without him putting walls up.

It could very well backfire epically.

I wasn't under any grand illusions that my plan would make Spencer fall in love with me.

But it was a way to allow him to keep me in the friend-zone *and* help me, which was something he always wanted to do. Selfishly, it would also give me something that I'd never get otherwise—Spencer in a *more-than-friends* situation. At least for a little bit.

I closed my eyes and sighed. The plan wasn't foolproof. Not even close.

I wasn't going to flat-out lie to Spencer. More like exaggerate the truth and—if Spencer took me up on my plan—enjoy a temporary situation that I'd never get for real. I prided myself on usually being rational and intelligent, but the craving I had for Spencer had overruled all of that.

I just needed Spencer to agree to my plan.

"Aww, look at this guy," Spencer said as he held up a crocheted rainbow unicorn. "It's like the one in that book you were reading to Hadley."

I smiled. Hadley had kinda adopted me and Spencer as her reading buddies whenever she was at

Bev's. Which was adorable because Spencer was a cute mixture of awed by the kid and terrified of her. But whenever she asked for him to read a book, it was as if her every wish was his command. "So cute. We should get it for her."

"How much?" Spencer asked the individual at the little craft table in the game store.

"Twenty. Cash or Venmo," they answered cheerily.

"Shit, I don't have cash." Spencer pulled his phone out. "I can do Venmo, though."

"Oh, here. I still owe you that ten dollars. Let me send it to you and that way we can split the payment." I clicked around on my phone and sent the ten back to Spencer.

A couple moments later, he had the plush in a plastic bag as we continued to look around the store.

"So, this is where your gaming group plays?" Spencer asked as he toyed with some dice.

"Yeah, I don't join them as often as they get together, but I've been coming down here a couple times a week." Being able to have a little bit of freedom to just be *me* rather than drowning in work, money, and housing issues had been such a refreshing change.

"What do you play? Is it video games or RPG?"

I pointed to a few of the back rooms. "I mostly

play Dungeons and Dragons if I'm looking to play a tabletop RPG. Some people like to play Pathfinder, Shadowrun, Call of Cthulhu, things like that."

"You ever play the console or laptop games?"

"Yeah, I have. Usually I'll join in on Borderlands if there's a group playing. I have a crappy laptop for school, definitely not made for gaming, so if the shop has Borderlands playing on Xbox or PlayStation, I'll play if there's room."

"I've played that some with Cooper and Dalton. It's fun. We usually just play Call of Duty, Mortal Kombat, Dead by Daylight," Spencer said. "I never really got into the tabletop games."

"I like them all for different reasons. Tabletop is just fun for me because it makes me feel like I'm using my brain more." I shrugged. "It's been really nice having time to relax and play at home or down here at the shop." I picked up a pack of cards I'd been eyeing, but froze.

I sensed him before I saw him because the hairs on the back of my neck stood up. "Well, it must be my lucky day," a smarmy voice cooed from behind me. "I didn't know you were coming in today, Raiden. Want to get a private game going?"

I gritted my teeth and turned to face Lance even as Spencer bristled at my side. "Hey, Lance. Didn't come to play, just showing Spencer around."

The way Lance's eyes traveled up and down my body made me want to puke. The guy was probably my closest competition in school and could have been a fun friend to have in the gaming group, but his aggressive flirting and overt come-ons ever since he'd transferred in were just too much.

He gave a dismissive glance toward Spencer before giving me a smile that was anything but kind. "Your *friend* can go home. I'll give you a ride later. Let's hang. Maybe head back to my place for a while?"

Ugh, this was a large part of why I needed Spencer to go for my plan. Lance didn't seem to take my subtle hints that I wasn't interested; if Spencer would help me out, maybe Lance would get a clue.

"Nah, he's good," Spencer said gruffly, moving slightly in front of me as if acting as a shield. "I'm Spencer and you're?"

Lance sneered. "Lance. Classmate and gaming buddy. It's no problem, I can give him a ride. You look like you don't exactly want to be here. Let Raiden hang with his buddies."

"I'm good," I interrupted. "Spencer and I have plans." I gave a silent prayer that Spencer would go along with what I was saying.

"Yeah, in fact, we better get going," Spencer added.

Grateful to Spencer for jumping right into the farce, I gave Lance a little wave. "See you in class."

"Are you going on the ski trip?" Lance asked, his eyes narrowed and calculating.

"Um, I'm thinking about it."

"It pays to be seen with the cohort. The teachers are looking for leaders and those who work well with the team. You should make sure you're there." He smirked and gave a wink that made me feel like I needed to shower. "I'll be sure to save you a seat next to me on the lift. I bet the hot tub is great for sore muscles after a long day on the slopes."

"Yeah, we'll see," I stammered before hightailing it out of the shop, thankful for Spencer's presence by my side.

"Who the hell was that?" he demanded once we were on the sidewalk.

I shuddered. "Lance. He's new in my classes and started coming to the game shop a few weeks ago."

"He's interested, that's for sure." Spencer shot me a look. "Is the feeling mutual?"

"Ugh, not at all. I keep trying to give subtle hints, but it's not working."

"Yeah, he seems like the type of asshole who needs beat over the head with *No* and even then, he might not get it." Spencer yanked open his truck door. "What's the ski trip he's talking about?"

After climbing in, I took a deep breath. I hadn't planned on today being the day I proposed my possibly disastrous plan to Spencer, but the opening had presented itself and I couldn't turn it down. "Now that the cohort at school has been whittled down to a core group, they start planning trips and outings to build camaraderie and leadership skills. The first trip is to Midwest Snow next weekend. They've reserved a block of rooms—super cheap because it's not their prime season and one of the girls in class knows the owner—and we're invited to spend the weekend."

"Are you going?" Spencer asked as he pulled into the restaurant where we'd decided earlier we'd eat lunch.

Once we were seated, I shrugged. "I want to go because it will look bad if I don't go. But I don't want to put up with Lance."

"Yeah, I can see that. He's a smarmy asshole."

We placed our drink orders.

I cleared my throat. "We're friends, right?"

Spencer frowned. "Of course. Why?"

"Well, I have a really big favor to ask you. Like *huge*." I rubbed my sweaty palms on my jeans. "I know you *just* got me a place to live and I shouldn't even be asking you this, but you're kinda the only person I trust enough to ask."

"What? You're kinda freakin' me out."

"I was wondering if you'd want to maybe kinda be my fake boyfriend around Lance? Get him to believe we're together so he'll back off? I mean, it wouldn't have to be all the time, just let him see us together a few times and see if he gets the hint?"

Spencer's eyes went wide. "Where would he see us together?"

I winced. "I was thinking you could go on the ski trip with me? And there's a gaming trip in a couple weeks. Maybe a couple appearances at the shop? I think there may be a cohort dinner coming up." I bit my lip. "I'm thinking if he sees us together and thinks we're an item, he'll maybe move his attention to someone else?"

I wasn't sure exactly what I was expecting from Spencer, but waiting for him to respond was torture.

He took a really deep breath as he stared at me. Then he huffed as he pinched the bridge of his nose and closed his eyes.

"Sorry, it's a really stupid idea. I'll just keep telling him no. And I won't go on the ski trip if he hasn't gotten that I'm not into him that way." I fiddled with the salt shaker.

"No, I'm not saying no. Just trying to wrap my head around it. You think Lance would even believe we're together?" Spencer cocked his head. "He seemed to pick up pretty quickly that the game shop wasn't my normal hangout."

I smiled and nudged his foot. "Your normal hangout is on a roof, at the diner, playing video games, or relaxing in bed," I teased. "I don't know that he *knew* you weren't the type to be there or if he was just hoping to get you to go away."

We paused long enough to get our drinks and place our food order for pizza and breadsticks.

"Don't you think he'll wonder what in the hell we're doing together?"

I winced, but swallowed the hurt and barreled on. "I mean, I'm sure he'll question how I lucked out to get a guy like you, but if we play it up convincingly enough, it should work. Once he backs off and moves on, we can do a quiet, fake break-up and you'll be off the hook."

"I meant he'd probably wonder why *you'd* be with *me*," Spencer grumbled. "Maybe you should find someone who would be more your type?"

I shook my head. I *definitely* didn't want to try to fake a relationship with anyone but Spencer. One, I trusted him. Two, I was so hooked on him, I couldn't stop thinking that fake boyfriends would *maybe* need to practice kissing and holding hands if we were to pull off the charade. But I had to get him to agree first. "I've never really dated, definitely don't have the experience to make me confident enough to try to pull this off with anyone but you. You're the only person I'd trust."

Spencer leaned forward and put his head in his hands.

"You can say no. I'd get it. But I'm trying to not get a complex; I know you'd never go for me in real life." I worried my lip. "But is it really that terrible?"

His eyes widened and he shook his head. "No, not at all. I'm not against helping you and we get along great, so it shouldn't be too hard to convince Lance. I just don't want to mess anything up." He pursed his lips. "And I guess I'm kinda wondering how far you're thinking the fake relationship needs to go?"

I waited for the pizza to be placed on the table before answering. "Nothing will get messed up. You're easily my best friend. In some ways, you're my only friend. I mean, I count Cooper and Jesse and everyone else at Remington Place, but I promise we'll stay friends." I had to take a drink of my soda to hide the uncertainty in my voice. Could I really promise that Spencer and I could keep our friendship after we faked being boyfriends? It would be easy for Spencer to go back to being just my friend, sure. But for me? Being in love with my best friend was hard enough. Getting to have him as a boyfriend, even if just in my imagination and for show, was going to wreck me. Would *I* be able to flip the switch and go back to being just friends?

I cleared my throat. I'd have to. There was no other option because I wasn't losing Spencer.

We each ate for a few moments before Spencer took a drink and continued the conversation. "And what about how far you think the whole fake thing needs to go?"

All the way I wanted to say. I wanted touching, kissing, dirty words, sex...I wanted it all.

Instead, my cheeks heated as I answered, "Hadn't really thought about it. Figured I needed you to agree first." I shrugged. "Maybe we play it by ear and take it as far as it seems to need to go so Lance will move on?"

"What about people at home? Tell them? Let them know it's fake or let them think it's real?" Spencer asked around a bite of breadstick.

I thought about that for a moment. "I think we let them in on it. I don't see any reason why they'd ever need to meet Lance, but if they know what's going on, they can play it up for us. Just in case."

Spencer nodded.

We sat quietly while he drummed his fingers on the table.

"And it's just us for however long the fake thing

needs to go on?" he finally asked. "I mean, I've never dated, but I'm pretty sure I'd want my fake boyfriend to be monogamous," he said with a teasing wink.

"Yeah, we're in a committed, serious, fake relationship for sure," I answered with a chuckle.

"Guess I'll need to know the dates for all these outings so I can be sure I'm not working," Spencer finally said.

I'd hoped against hope, but I really hadn't been sure if he'd agree. "You'll do it? For real?"

"You know I can't say no to you. I'd do whatever it takes to help you," Spencer said with pink cheeks and a lift of his shoulder.

We finished up lunch and headed home.

As we climbed the stairs to our room, I decided to press my luck. "Want to figure out the dates so you can check your schedule?"

"Yeah," Spencer answered gruffly. "Probably better make sure my wardrobe is appropriate too. Blue collar duds don't usually work for anything more than getting dirty."

"And working hard to build safe, reliable housing for people," I added. "You'll never convince me that you're anything less than amazing—I don't care what your job title is. You're good at it and it helps people. Period."

By the time dinner rolled around, Spencer and I

had synced our calendars for at least three official school or gaming functions where we'd for sure see Lance along with penciling in a couple trips to the shop.

"I'm going to need new clothes," Spencer muttered.

"Same, at least for the dinner thing. We can go shopping," I suggested.

When Spencer looked as if he'd rather chew off his arm, I laughed and patted his shoulder. "It won't be *that* bad."

Spencer grumbled.

"We can ask Cooper and Jesse to go with us," I said as we walked into the kitchen.

"Ask Cooper and Jesse to go with you? Where are we going?" Cooper asked as he gave Bev a hug.

Everyone began to fill their plates, but it seemed I had the floor. "Oh, um." I shot a look to Spencer and he nodded. "Well, there's this guy at school who isn't taking the hint that I don't like him. Spence has agreed to be my fake boyfriend around this guy just until he backs off. We need to go shopping for some dress clothes for a dinner and I thought maybe you and Jesse would like to go?"

Wide eyes filled the room.

Jesse and Cooper smiled.

Bev chuckled and shook her head. "Here we go again," she muttered.

Dalton scoffed. "You gonna fake make out?" Gabby shushed him.

Dre smirked. "Sounds like a *great* plan. Let me know how it works out."

Spencer bristled. "Look, I met this guy. Lance. He's a douche. Rai needs my help." He sat his plate on the table with a bit more force than was necessary and took his seat. "Maybe it's not the best plan in the world, but if it gets the asshole to back off, it's worth it. It's not going to hurt Rai or me in anyway."

"Have you tried just telling the guy you're not interested?" Dalton asked.

The table was full and everyone had started eating. Dalton's question wasn't accusatory, but I still felt defensive. Had I been direct enough with Lance? Or was I so into the idea of faking it with Spencer that I went straight to that option?

I nodded. "He doesn't seem to care. I've told him no several times. About hanging out in private, going on dates, going back to his place. He just keeps at it."

"He's also pretty aggressive from what I saw," Spencer added. "He came across sort of like a kid who wants a specific toy. Wants it, wants it, wants it, and won't stop until he gets it." He shrugged.

"Maybe if he sees someone else has the toy, he'll get distracted by something else and focus his attention there."

"So, what do you need dress clothes for?" Cooper asked. "And just a side note, we'll definitely go shopping with you. I need new jeans. We can go on a double-date."

"Is it really a double-date if half the group is fake dating?" Dre teased.

"You wouldn't need new jeans if you'd stop buying the ones that are already ripped to shreds," Dalton said with a roll of his eyes.

I'd grown accustomed to—and very fond of—the banter at the table, so I took it in stride. "At school, the cohort is pretty much set now. In the beginning, the group was much larger, but it's been whittled down. Some people had to drop out, some transferred, some needed a different schedule—I was close to having to take a break myself, so again, thanks to all of you for letting me live here." I tore a piece from a roll and popped it in my mouth. "Anyway, now that the cohort is set, we'll start doing outings and functions to build teamwork and leadership. We're going on a ski trip first."

"I figure I have enough outdoor work gear to do that one without much trouble. I think we can rent boots and skis," Spencer said, but he glanced my way. "I've never been skiing. You?"

I shook my head. "We'll stay on the bunny slope."

"Don't even think about breaking anything," Bev warned with a wave of her fork.

"Then there's a dinner function at the school. It's like a meet the staff, meet the families of your classmates, get your name out there for future reference, that type thing," I explained. "We *both* need to get some clothes for that. I had some dress clothes when I left home, but I've grown since then."

"When did you want to go?" Jesse asked. "I could probably do Saturday after a few morning appointments at the shop."

"That works," I said.

"Perfect. We'll make a day of it." Cooper glanced toward the little girl sitting next to Jesse. "Hadley, do you want to see if Mandy can babysit or ask Ms. Bev?"

Hadley beamed at the older woman sitting next to her. "Ms. Bev, please."

Bev leaned over and kissed her head. "Of course, my dear. We'll have to bake something. You be thinking of what you'd like."

With that settled, the meal continued with easy

chatter until we cleared the dishes and Bev started coffee and tea.

"I've got shortbread cookies for dessert," she said.

Within twenty minutes, Dre had taken a travel mug of coffee and a stack of cookies so he could head to a shift—he was working as an EMT in addition to trying to get his fashion line off the ground.

Dalton and Gabby had given Bev hugs and headed upstairs with their coffee and cookies. I'd been there long enough now to know those two loved their family, but they also worked hard to keep their private time sacred. Maybe it had something to do with how many hours they both put in at their office jobs, but they seemed to make it a priority to turn off work and focus on just them when they were home.

Bev had a show she wanted to watch, so she gave hugs and headed to her room.

Which left Hadley, Cooper, Jesse, Spencer, and me in the living room.

"Oh," Spencer started. "Hadley, Rai and I got you something." He rushed up the stairs and came back down with his hand behind his back. "Probably should have wrapped it," he said sheepishly.

Hadley closed her eyes and held out her hand.

Spencer placed the rainbow unicorn in her waiting hands.

She opened her eyes and squealed as if it was the best gift she'd ever gotten. "I love it! It's just like in the book. Thank you." Hadley gave me a hug and then Spencer.

I couldn't help but smile at how Spencer seemed so proud that Hadley liked her gift and so terrified that she was hugging him.

"Can we read that book again?" Hadley asked and rushed to the book basket Bev kept for her.

"Oh, that reminds me. I was going through my boxes and found some books I smuggled from my room when I left. I have some Japanese storybooks. I'll put them in the basket. We can read some of my favorites if you'd like," I told Hadley.

"Yes! I want to hear Japanese stories. Can you *talk* in Japanese?" Hadley held the unicorn book.

"I know a bit. My parents and grandparents spoke it almost exclusively at home with each other, but my parents spoke English with me in hopes that I'd learn and fit in at school." I smiled when Spencer took his place on the loveseat—Hadley had him trained well—and I took my spot beside him so Hadley could climb up on his lap. "I can't read Japanese at all—there are three alphabets. I can understand some spoken Japanese, but there are several dialects of the language so it's not all easy for me to understand. I've likely lost a lot of it over the years."

"That's okay. I forget things sometimes, too," Hadley said as she handed the book to me. "Take turns," she instructed.

I began to read. If the book was at Hadley's level, we'd let her read to us and help when she got stuck, but she seemed to often pick books that were a bit more challenging so the grownups could read to her. She was a great reader already and Cooper said having the more challenging stories read to her would actually help her in the long run.

So, Spencer and I passed the book back and forth as we read about the rainbow unicorn that helped two friends and saved the day while Hadley played with the plush toy we'd bought her.

Cooper and Jesse cuddled on the couch looking cute as could be, but when the story was over, they were quick to call it a night. I'd learned from comments and secret glances that after Hadley's bedtime was Cooper and Jesse time.

So sweet.

I sighed as they headed over to Jesse's house.

I wanted a special time.

With Spencer.

"You heading to bed?" he asked.

"Yeah, gonna shower first. Unless you wanted to go first?"

"We could fake shower together," he quipped, but then his eyes grew wide and his cheeks pinked. "Joking, totally joking." He cleared his throat. "You go ahead. I'm beat, may not even shower until morning if I fall asleep before you're done."

We made our way upstairs with a heavy awkwardness between us.

Spencer flopped onto his bed and I rushed to the bathroom.

Had I made a terrible mistake? Were we now doomed to awkward weirdness all because of the fake boyfriends thing?

Shit.

I soaped up and rinsed. Had I been stupid in thinking that faking it would at least give me an excuse to maybe kiss Spencer? Was it worth that chance if it meant losing the easy friendship we'd had?

I couldn't lose Spencer.

But I also couldn't stop thinking about what it would be like to kiss him, to feel his hands on me, to touch his body.

My cock was totally into the idea and I knew there was no way I could go back to our room with a rock-hard erection. Closing my eyes, my hand slick with conditioner, I stroked myself while imagining Spencer's kisses, his fist gripping me, and me on my knees sucking him off. I came hard and fast. I didn't have experience to back me up—and I knew the porn I watched wasn't realistic—but I wanted so many things with Spencer.

Would he ever give in and let me have what I craved?

"ARE you sure this is a good idea?" Jesse asked quietly as he popped a bite of soft pretzel in his mouth while we followed Cooper and Spencer through the mall.

The two friends seemed deep in conversation ahead of us, and I figured it was good for Spencer to get some quality time with Cooper. From what I could tell, Coop and Spencer had been inseparable for about three years while living with Bev. Then Jesse had moved in next door, swept Cooper off his feet—completely unplanned and maybe it was the other way around—and Spencer had kinda lost his bestie.

Not that he begrudged Cooper his happiness, but I knew Spencer missed having Cooper around as much as he used to be. Between Cooper being at

Jesse's almost one hundred percent of the time *and* busy running the new preschool he'd opened—the *very* successful preschool, I might add—Cooper and Spencer didn't get their friend time as much.

And I kinda felt guilty knowing that *I* was part of that equation as well. I hadn't thought of it until right at that moment, but I'd pretty much waltzed into Spencer's life and took up his time as well.

"Earth to Raiden," Jesse teased.

I pulled myself from the thoughts and refocused on what he'd asked me as I chewed my pretzel. "A good idea?" I mumbled. "Fudge if I know."

Jesse smirked. "Look, I get that. I went into the whole thing with Cooper knowing it was a terrible idea but completely unable to say no to him. I think the key to your situation is to communicate. Don't assume Spencer knows how you're feeling. *Talk* to him."

"What do you mean *how I'm feeling*?" I narrowed my eyes.

Jesse stared at me for a moment. "I get the feeling that this fake dating thing is kinda a ruse to get close to Spencer? Maybe sort of push him into something he maybe wouldn't have acted on on his own?"

My eyes went wide and I started to argue, but then my shoulders sagged. "Is it *that* obvious?"

Jesse chuckled.

"For real though," I gestured with my pretzel, "there really is a douchebag asshole named Lance who won't take no for an answer. It's not like I'm making that part up."

Taking another bite, Jesse smiled while he chewed. "Well, at least you don't have a fake admirer along with your fake boyfriend. So, what's your endgame? Aside from getting Lance to back off?"

"Endgame?"

"Like your goal. What are you hoping happens with this plan?"

I swallowed thickly. "I guess I want Lance to back off and I get to spend time with Spencer in ways I normally wouldn't. Once Lance moves on, we'll go back to being friends."

Jesse laughed loudly enough that Spencer and Cooper glanced back at us suspiciously. "Sorry," he held a hand over his mouth while he finished chewing his food, "I just have first-hand experience with the whole *go back to being friends* game. It doesn't work."

"Spencer is my best friend. I can't lose him. I'm going to enjoy the hell out of the fake boyfriend thing, but he doesn't want me as more than a friend so I'll have no choice but to go back to the way things were."

Jesse studied me as we walked. "So, your situation is different than mine in some ways. Cooper and I were doing the whole *just sex and then we walk away* thing and it didn't go as planned. *You're* looking for just putting on a show for Lance. Are you wanting things between you and Spencer to go deeper than just a surface dating game?"

I bit my lip and nodded. "You won't tell him, right? I *know* that Spencer would *never* go for me; I'm not his type at all."

"Does Spencer *have* a type?" Jesse wondered aloud.

"I know it's stupid and selfish. I'm being greedy and probably setting myself up for a terrible heartache. But I can't help thinking that maybe Spencer can show me a few things—he knows I'm inexperienced. Maybe I can convince him to teach me some things while we're faking it for Lance?" The pretzel suddenly tasted like sawdust. "Dumb, I know. But I can't help it, the guy makes me lose my mind."

Jesse grinned, but his eyes were on Cooper as he spoke. "I get it. Completely." He wadded up his pretzel bag and tossed it in the trash. "And you think Spencer would balk if you just asked him to do the whole friends-with-benefits thing?"

I gave Jesse a *duh* look and he chuckled. "Spencer

is convinced that he's not worthy of anyone or anything. I think he almost thinks just sharing a room with him is harming me and my future in some way. He'd never just agree to sex for the purpose of me losing my virginity."

"Okay, yeah, I see that." Jesse took a sip of his soda. "So, what makes you think he'll agree to it under the guise of fake dating?"

"He might not. The main point of the fake dating is to get rid of Lance. I'm just hopeful that maybe in the course of practice kissing and whatnot, that Spencer will maybe give in and let himself enjoy— even if just for a little bit." I winced. "I'm likely going to hell, but I was hoping maybe his usual inability to say no to me will carry over into the bedroom?"

Jesse took a deep breath. "So, let me make sure I've got this right. You're going to fake date. Which will inevitably lead to the need to kiss, touch, maybe make out. Then you're hoping to get Spencer to go further with all of that—kinda like a *we're already here, we might as well enjoy ourselves* type thing—and then, once Lance goes on his merry way, you and Spencer will just leave the kissing and touching and sex behind and go back to being friends. Is that the gist of it?"

I grimaced. "Well, when you put it that way, it

sounds doubly stupid and selfish. But, yes." I tossed the rest of my pretzel in a trashcan as we walked. "I promise I'd never make Spencer do anything he doesn't want to do."

Smirking, Jesse shook his head. "I don't think that will be a problem. I just think the two of you are going into this thinking you can walk out the other side with no consequences. I don't know if that's possible."

"You won't tell him any of this, right?" I asked. "My main goal is get rid of Lance, enjoy some time with Spencer that he'd never agree to otherwise, and then go back to being friends."

"I have no reason to meddle in your business. I'd only tell Spencer if I thought either of you were in danger. But if he were to ask me, I'd definitely tell him that I think the two of you should give up on the *fake* part and just see where the mutual attraction takes you."

I scoffed. "*Mutual?* Yeah, right. You know Spencer thinks himself not worthy of happiness."

"Spencer's self-perception has nothing to do with whether he finds you attractive. Now, it may affect whether he allows himself to *act* on that attraction, but I don't think lack of attraction is your biggest problem." Jesse glanced toward where Cooper and Spencer had entered a store. "Just keep in mind that being open and honest is your best bet—believe me, I'm speaking from experience. Spencer needs to accept that he deserves happiness, but *you* also need to accept the same. I'd like to think you'll both eventually figure out that your happiness is in each other and you're both worthy of it."

I processed Jesse's words and smiled softly. "Maybe that's my true endgame, but my past has taught me to just take the bits and pieces of good that come my way because I may never get the whole thing."

Jesse pressed his lips together as if biting back something he wanted to say. "We better find the boys before Cooper buys seven pairs of jeans that look exactly the same but he swears they're all unique and needed."

I chuckled. "Yeah, and I need dinner wear."

We walked into the store. The talk with Jesse had helped, but it had also brought some heaviness to the forefront of my mind.

I was too selfish to give up this chance with Spencer—plus, I *did* want to get rid of Lance—but I worried for the outcome of our friendship.

Fudge. I *really* hoped I wasn't setting myself and Spencer up for a major crash and burn.

SIX
SPENCER

"So, fake dating, huh?" Cooper asked as we walked toward a store.

"He's a friend, he needed help. That's all," I answered gruffly.

"Spence, *I'm* a friend. And I'm pretty sure you never would have agreed to fake date me even if I'd needed help." Cooper cocked a brow and waited.

I scowled and started to argue, but he wasn't completely wrong. "Fake dating might involve some fake kissing and I can't bring myself to even think about kissing you; you're like my brother." I shivered as he laughed.

"So, you've at least thought about the fact that you might need to get up close and personal in order to pull off this charade?"

"Sure. And if it gets Lance to leave Rai alone, I'm all for it," I grumbled.

"And that's the only reason you're doing this? *Just* to help Raiden with the Lance issue?" Cooper's knowing eyes studied me.

Jesse's loud laughter behind us drew our attention. I liked that Jesse and Rai were getting along; Rai needed more friends than just me.

"Of course I want to help Rai. That's why I'm doing this."

"But is it the *only* reason?" Cooper pressed.

I took a deep breath. Cooper was my best friend and I knew I could trust him with my life. "I know it's wrong, okay? I get that. But I'd be lying if I said the selfish bastard part of me wasn't looking forward to whatever time this fake dating thing buys me with Rai."

"You really like him, huh?" Cooper's words were soft and understanding.

"Have you seen him? Talked to him? What's not to like? He's gorgeous, smart, fun, and we can spend time together without ever running out of things to do or say even if we're just sitting there doing and saying nothing." I ran my hand over my face.

"Why not just date for real then?" Cooper asked.

I scoffed. "Yeah, right. Raiden Ono, future nurse and humanitarian, with Spencer Nelson, construction worker and dud. No way. He deserves more than me and whatever dull future I might have."

"Stop." He held up a hand. "One day, I hope you realize how good and worthy you are. You deserve love and happiness as much as Rai does. As much as *anyone* does." Cooper cocked his head with a soft smile. "Maybe eventually you'll both believe that." He waved off my protest. "So, you think real dating would be bad. Gotcha." He wagged his finger my direction. "Just want to be sure we remember this day later. When you and Rai are madly in love and building your future together, I want it noted that I suggested a real relationship first."

"Like the real relationship you started with Jesse in the beginning?" I deadpanned.

Cooper pursed his lips. "Just trying to save you from the consequences I had to suffer. *Anyway*, how exactly are you thinking you'll deal with all that fake dating entails without falling for Rai?"

"Well, that ship has done sailed," I mumbled, throwing a glance over my shoulder to take in the beautiful form of Rai gesturing with his pretzel while chatting with Jesse. "But I'll deal. Number one goal is help Rai out of the Lance situation. As long as that happens, it's a win. Any extra time or touching we might get from it is just icing on the cake."

Cooper waggled his brow as we walked into the store. "So, you're open to showing Rai his way around bedroom fun?"

I growled. "Kissing. Touching. I'm not going to maul him or take advantage. I'm sure he'd rather save that for someone who means more to him than a fake boyfriend."

"And if he sees his fake boyfriend as someone he cares for and trusts and *wants* to be the one who teaches him?" Cooper cocked a brow and pursed his lips.

"First, he won't."

"Humor me," Cooper fingered a rack of shirts.

"I'd like to think I could be the good guy and keep things to just kissing and some touching." My gut clenched and my cock stirred at the thought of even just kisses and touches with Rai.

"And if Rai—being of sound mind and body and completely able to make decisions for himself— suggests that he wants his deflowering to take place at *your* hands?"

I choked on air and glanced toward the door to make sure Rai and Jesse hadn't arrived yet. "Jesus, Coop." I shook my head. "Don't say things like that."

"You haven't answered the question."

I pinched the bridge of my nose. "I'd do my best to convince him that he should wait."

"So, you'd rather Rai learn with someone—maybe someone as shitty as Lance—than to learn in the arms of his trusted best friend?" Cooper batted his lashes.

"Fuck, no," I growled.

Cooper just chuckled and shook his head. "This situation is going to be fun to watch. Mark my words. The fake dating is going to feel so right and so perfect, you'll wonder how you ever lived without Rai in your life."

Too late, already wonder that.

Cooper continued. "The practice kissing and touching will light you on fire. Rai's pleading whimpers to please show him more, teach him, be the first to touch him that way will go straight to your dick *and* your heart. You already can't say no to him. Just wait until you're drunk on his kisses, his eager lips and fingers longing to learn what turns you on," he whisper-teased suggestively.

"Fuck off, Coop. Stop talking like that." I yanked a shirt off the rack. "This isn't some fantasy dream. This is real life. Rai doesn't like me that way and it's for the best. I'm going to help *a friend* and we'll stay friends. Period."

Cooper smirked. "Oh, I didn't say anything about

not staying friends. Isn't there some kind of saying? Friends who suck cock together stay together or something like that?"

"Jesus, Coop. Keep your voice down." My friend had zero filter and the middle of a clothing store wasn't where I wanted to be talking about sucking cock. *Especially* when the cocks and mouths in question happened to be mine and Rai's—something I'd had a *very* hard time keeping *out* of my mind lately.

"Look, all I'm saying is that Jesse and I are friends *and* burning up the sheets. You and Rai can do the same. Just let it happen." Cooper elbowed me. "Get out of your head—stop believing all of the lies you've told yourself all these years. You deserve love and happiness. *Rai* deserves love and happiness. Give this thing a chance and see what happens. Maybe you'll both end up with what you deserve."

I wanted so badly to believe that.

But my head started in. *You're nothing. You'll never be anything. You came from nothing. You're going nowhere. Don't strap him to your nothingness.*

No, I'd help Rai because he was my friend and needed me. Maybe I'd get a few selfish moments where he and I got to experience *more* than just friendship. But then, I'd go back to being his friend. That's all I deserved to be.

My heart clenched as Rai and Cooper headed off to a display of dress clothes. I could be his friend. No problem. Being in love with him from afar? Getting the tiniest taste of him and then letting him go? Watching him move on with someone who could make him happy? Those things just might kill me.

"They're quite the pair, huh?" Jesse asked from beside me.

"Definitely. Can't wait to see what they end up picking out. I'm hoping I can get away with black pants, dark shirt, simple tie. Pretty sure my dusty-ass work boots aren't going to pass the test, though." I glanced toward the shoe section.

"You know that Cooper and I—everyone at Bev's really—we're all on your side and want nothing but the best for you and Raiden, right?" Jesse asked quietly.

"He deserves the best," I said, smiling as Rai held up a shirt for Cooper's critique.

"*You* deserve good things, too."

I shrugged. "Watching him be happy will have to be enough."

"Lousy timing and don't want to push too much," Jesse muttered as he reached into his pocket, "but you really need to give my therapist, Alicia, a call. She has great cookies and tea. She really helped me through a lot of what I was dealing with after Nicole and Lauren. She helped me with the whole Cooper thing too. Even if you and Rai don't end up as a situation, *you* owe it to yourself to talk to a professional. God knows hearing it from your friends hasn't started to sink in."

I took the card and shoved it into my pocket. "I'll think about it." I probably wouldn't. The therapists I'd worked with as a kid and teen hadn't been helpful, what would make this one any different?

Maybe you're older now? Maybe you've had a chance to see things from a different perspective? Maybe because even just the slight chance that talking to her would make things possible with Rai?

I'd think about it.

By the time we arrived back at Remington Place, purchases in hand, I was exhausted.

"Pretty sure that shopping with Cooper should be limited to once or twice a year." I put my bags on the floor and flopped onto my bed. "Don't think I could survive many more trips like that. I love that guy, but damn, between his mouth, his constant *go go go*, and his insistence that I try on every damn piece of clothing he deemed necessary, I'm pretty sure I could sleep for days."

"I will say," Rai chuckled as he placed his bags on the desk and rolled onto his bed, "I think I'll have to better prepare for the next shopping trip with him. He's relentless."

I'd ended up with black dress pants, two dark dress shirts, two coordinating ties, and black shoes. Oh, and dress socks. Seemed like a waste, but even I realized that my thick white work socks wouldn't mesh with the look.

While I'd insisted Cooper stick to a fairly classic look for my new clothes, he and Rai had seemed to have fun building a trendier look for Rai. He'd ended up with two pairs of black pants—one plain and one with a shimmer—a pale lilac colored shirt, a teal one, one long tie and one bow tie, a pair of black dress shoes, and a pair of black dress boots. I hadn't seen all of the complete outfits *on* Rai, but I knew he'd look like a damn super model just stepping off the runway in them.

"You're happy with your purchases?" I asked, my eyes closed and arm draped across my head.

Rai sighed. "Very. Until you and this place, I'd never had the opportunity to go shopping just for fun. I mean, I know we needed the clothes for the events, but in the past, I would have ended up at a thrift shop hoping to find something that wasn't too worn." He rolled to face me. "Today was fun. Thanks for going."

"No problem." The card in my pocket poked at

me when I shifted. Pulling it out, I stared at the name.

"What's that?"

I tossed the card onto the nightstand between our beds. "The name of Jesse's therapist. He sings her praises—I guess she really helped him through some stuff when he moved here—and thinks I should go see her."

"And what do you think?"

Curling onto my side, I sighed heavily. "I think that no therapists in my past helped me."

"Maybe you weren't at a point where you were ready for the help?" Rai asked quietly.

I grunted. "I think that maybe I'm too messed up for some talking to help me."

"I don't know. I usually feel better after a good talk."

"And maybe," I said softly, hating my vulnerability, "maybe it's scary as fuck to think about telling her all about me."

Rai stood and walked to my bed. The mattress dipped as he sat beside me, his hand resting on my shoulder. "You've told *me* all about you and nothing went up in flames. Maybe it's also fudging scary to think that talking to her may help? It may take you out of the comfort zone you've built around yourself

—no matter how negative and harmful that comfort zone is."

"So, if you were as fucked up as me, you'd go see this therapist?" I spoke with my eyes closed, enjoying the warmth of Rai's hand on my shoulder.

"I've been thinking it would be good for *me* to speak to someone for quite a while. Our pasts are different, but we both have some issues to work through." Rai squeezed my shoulder. "What if we make a deal?"

I cracked open one eye. "What kind of deal?"

"We'll both go see," Rai leaned over and picked up the card, "Alicia. Agree to at least three meetings with her and then we can reassess."

"Do you think she'd allow us to come together for our first meeting? I know it sounds stupid—especially for someone who has been on his own basically his whole life—but going to meet a therapist alone for the first time is really scary." God, I was such a loser.

"I say we tell her that's the way we're doing it. Once we've met her, we can set up our own sessions, but there's nothing wrong with wanting a supportive friend with you for something like this." Rai pocketed the card. "Can I take care of calling and setting up our first meeting?"

I drew in a deep breath and let it out slowly.

"Three sessions and then we can stop if it's not working?"

Rai nodded, his dark brown eyes locked on mine.

"Okay. I'm in. But don't expect for any miracles to occur. I'm sure I'll still be the same fucked up mess." I snuggled into my pillow. I was so damn tired of feeling like such a waste.

"We can be fudged up messes together," Rai said lightly as he stood. "I think Bev said dinner would be ready in about twenty minutes."

"Just need a short nap," I mumbled.

"Can we talk about something after?" Rai asked.

"Sure thing," I answered, my words slurred as I fell asleep.

The nap did me a world of good and I felt much better throughout dinner with my friends—no, the people of Remington Place were *family*. Found family, chosen family, whatever you wanted to call them. But family all the same.

Once we'd eaten, visited, and cleaned up, Rai and I made our way back to our room. Despite the nap to keep me going, I was running on fumes and definitely wanted bed over video games that night.

"Gonna shower," I told Rai. "Then we can talk about whatever you wanted."

He nodded and mumbled something I couldn't hear.

Thirty minutes later, we'd both taken quick showers and were hanging up our new clothes.

"So, what did you want to talk about?" I asked.

"Oh, um, it's probably stupid and you can say no," Rai stammered, his cheeks an adorable pink.

I hated that Rai was possibly the smartest person I'd ever met, and so confident in his academics and even in game play, but when it came to having confidence in *Rai*, he was sorely lacking. I moved to stand directly in front of him. "Nothing you say is stupid. And I know I can always say no." I smirked and bent to catch his eye. "But it seems I have a bit of trouble doing that when it comes to you. Whatever it is, I want to help."

"Well, um, the ski trip is coming up."

"Is it? I wasn't aware," I teased.

Rai huffed. "So, it's our first chance to be sure Lance sees us together and I figure we want to make it look good, right?"

I nodded. "Would make sense to be sure the first impression is a good one—and in our case, a *good* first impression means Lance believes we're a couple. Yeah, go on."

"Well, um, I figure it's kinda like preparing for a test, right? You can't expect to walk into the classroom and do well without some effort ahead of time." Rai closed his eyes and sighed. "I was thinking maybe we should practice with some couple-type stuff."

"Oh, like making sure we have our story straight? I mean, I'm guessing we go with as close to the truth as possible on that one. We met at the diner, got to be friends, you needed a place to stay, and the rest is history. No need to embellish it much—the more we fabricate, the harder it is to keep the story straight." In my gut, I *knew* that wasn't exactly what Rai was alluding to, but my brain and libido were moving into freak out, overload mode and I needed to buy some time.

Rai nodded. "Yeah, that's a good plan. And already being friends means we don't have to learn much about each other." He paused, shuffling a bit and seeming unsure how to continue.

"What else has you worried?" I was an asshole of epic proportions. I knew what had him worried. It was the same thing that had me in a knot of nerves. But I was going to make him spell it out, huh? Just to save myself from having to do the same?

Rai cleared his throat. "Um, like other couple-y stuff. Holding hands? Is that something we do? Or are we the no PDA at all type? I don't want to force you into something you don't want to do, and I know that you probably have a list of twenty people you'd rather do things with than me, but I guess I'm just wondering about the touching and…"

I reached for Rai's hand and pulled him closer. "I can deal with touching," I whispered, the connection between our hands buzzing like an electric current. "The more Lance sees us being all lovey-dovey, the better, right?"

Drawing his eyes from our joined hands, Rai's gaze caught mine. "And kissing," he blurted. Biting his lip, he continued, "I wondered about kissing. I don't have much experience and I'll likely suck at it, but maybe that's why we should practice. Lance might not believe it if we flounder, so practice may be our best bet," Rai's words trailed off breathlessly, his eyes wide as I pulled him even closer and cupped his cheek.

"Practice would probably be good," I murmured, my heart a violent drum solo against my chest.

"You don't have to. I feel like I'm making you do something you don't want to do," Rai whispered.

Rubbing a thumb over his lips, trying to memorize the silky smoothness of the pink skin, I silenced his words. With my mouth only a breath away, I closed my eyes, savoring the moment. "Kissing you will never be a hardship and *anyone* should count themselves lucky to get to do it."

Closing the space, bringing our lips together, I brushed a kiss over Rai's mouth.

Our first kiss should have stopped there.

After all, it was just for practice so Lance would believe we were together.

But the breathy little whimper that escaped Rai was too much and I was too weak.

I pulled him closer, deepening the kiss, thrilling in the press and glide of soft lips. When Rai's tongue darted out to tease, I opened for him. Our tongues met in an easy slip and slide, teasing and tasting, savoring and exploring.

Rai's arms came around my neck, our bodies melting together.

Wanting nothing more than to devour him, push him onto my bed and worship him, I forced myself to pull away. Panting, my forehead pressed to his and the taste of him still on my lips, I swallowed and worked to get myself under control.

You are so fucking screwed.

I'd known Rai would be the end of whatever sanity I had left. I'd known getting involved with him, even if just to help a friend, would ruin me. I'd *known* one taste of him would never be enough.

Yet I'd been powerless to stop it. I couldn't tell him no. Couldn't refuse to help him. And now, I was locked into a ski trip, holding hands, and kissing.

And what else? Would Rai want more the same way my body was screaming for more?

Why couldn't he have been a terrible kisser? Why couldn't our touches have felt as bland as rubbing my own arm?

Instead, Rai's touch had set me on fire. His kiss had made me feel alive.

And it was all just for show.

Cooper seems to think there's more to it than just faking it for Lance.

Even if there was more, Rai deserved more than what I could give him.

Ever think that maybe Rai should decide what he deserves?

No, we're friends and that's the way it has to be. We can do this whole fake thing, but then Rai needs to live his life without me pulling him down.

So, enjoy the time you have with him. Let yourself at least have that.

I closed my eyes and took a deep breath.

"Was that horrible?" Rai whispered. "I'm sorry. I don't have much to base it on, but I thought…"

I pressed a quick kiss against Rai's lips. "It wasn't horrible. It was really good, I'm impressed. I'm pretty sure Lance would fall for it."

A brief look of something passed over Rai's face, but he smiled. "Good. Mission accomplished. At least we have that part over with. Hand holding and kissing is a go."

I nodded. "Yep, good to go." I reluctantly let my hands fall from Rai's body and moved to my bed. How in the fuck was I supposed to get my first real taste of Rai and then go to sleep?

"I feel better about the ski trip, don't you?" Rai asked quietly from his side of the room.

"Yeah, good to have a plan," I answered.

The plan I really wanted—if I let myself imagine things I knew I couldn't have—would be Rai and me going on a trip together just because we wanted to. Kissing and touching whenever we felt like it, not just for show. And climbing into bed beside him to hold him as he slept.

That was the plan my heart and body wanted.

You've never gotten what you wanted, only the shit life you deserved, so you might as well prepare for the let down and heartache.

I curled onto my side, wishing I could block out reality and just revel in the memory of Rai's lips on mine.

Kissing him was going to be tempting enough, I *had* to be sure to avoid anything that went past kissing. I wasn't sure I could survive more than kissing with Rai and then give him up.

Sighing, sleep and worry warring with each other,

I wondered briefly before drifting off if I was strong enough to avoid the temptation of Rai. Sharing more than kisses with him and then going back to just friends would likely kill me. But never getting to experience everything I wanted to with him? I didn't know if I could live with that regret.

My only hope was that Rai wouldn't want to take things further than kissing. It was a reasonable hope. I had no reason to think he felt anything more than friendship towards me.

Did that kiss feel like a kiss between friends? Was the noise he made something you've ever heard a friend make around you?

I fell asleep torn between wanting Rai to be satisfied with kisses and hoping he wanted our fake relationship to go a few steps further.

Because I was a selfish bastard.

SEVEN
RAI

"I'LL GET the gas this round," Spencer said as he climbed from the truck.

I got out and stretched. We hadn't been driving long—Spencer had wanted to get started and stop for gas and coffee a bit farther down the road—but I wasn't the greatest at long trips. "I can get the coffee and snacks." We'd agreed to splitting the gas and food on the ski trip; I'd paid for the room myself since the trip was with my school group.

"I'll send you some money," he said as he pulled out his phone.

As I walked into the gas station, my phone buzzed with a notification of ten dollars sent from Spencer Nelson. I smiled. We'd basically been trading that ten dollars back and forth since we met.

I was in the snack aisle when Spencer joined me.

"I don't know what to get," I admitted. "Honestly, protein bars kept me alive and I should really show them some appreciation, but if I never eat another one again for as long as I live, it will be too soon."

"Chips, nuts, and chocolate are always a good bet," Spencer said. He picked up two cans of Pringles.

"Those aren't really *chips*, are they? I look at them as fake chips," I teased. I knew he had a thing for the canned chips and I had to give him a rough time.

"Fake chips for fake boyfriends. Perfect." Spencer winked.

"Fine. It's not like I don't enjoy them, I just think anything that looks that perfect can't claim to be a real chip." I picked up a bag of honey roasted peanuts.

"Oh, grab that bag of chocolate covered peanuts. Love those things and hardly ever remember to get any as a snack." Spencer gestured toward the rack of chocolate covered nuts.

"Not like we have much need for snacks at home; Bev keeps us pretty stocked." Remington Place was the first place I'd ever felt truly at home; even living with my blood family had never felt as comfortable and *right* as living with Bev and the crew.

"You want coffee?" Spencer asked.

"Yeah, and I'll grab waters," I told him.

"Four sugars and two creams?"

I smiled, loving that he knew my coffee preference. "Please."

By the time we loaded ourselves back into the truck, I was more at ease about the trip. If I could forget the fact that Lance would likely bring the awkwardness, the weekend could actually turn out to be fun.

No work, no school, and a road trip with my best friend? Could I really ask for more?

Don't forget the likelihood of holding hands and kissing.

I shivered at the memory of my hand in his, the press of his mouth against mine, the slide of our tongues, the lingering taste of him on my lips.

"You cold already? What am I going to do with you once we're on the snow?" Spencer teased as he popped a stack of Pringles into his mouth.

"Guess you'll have to keep me warm," I quipped before realizing how it sounded. "You know, for Lance. Make sure he knows I don't need him to warm me up," I blathered on like an idiot.

Spencer cleared his throat. "Yeah, we'll make it look good."

A couple hours later, we arrived at Midwest Snow and Spencer maneuvered his truck into one of the parking spots at the hotel.

After checking in, we lugged our bags to the room—grateful to be *renting* skis and boots rather than dealing with the cumbersome things. I swiped the key and walked into a bright, spacious room with Spencer right behind me.

"Wow, this is nice," I said, dropping the luggage and taking a look around. "I kinda thought since we got such a discounted price that the room would maybe be crappy, but I guess not."

Spencer still stood in the little entranceway hallway, bag on his shoulder, can of Pringles in hand.

"What's wrong? You don't like it?" I glanced around. "It seems clean, right?"

He nodded toward the middle of the room. "It's all good. Just hadn't been expecting…"

I looked to where his gaze was fixed on the bed.

The bed?

What was wrong with the bed?

Ohhh…

The bed.

As in *one* bed.

Fudge.

"Shit. One bed. I didn't even think. That's probably one of the reasons it was so much cheaper." I grimaced. "Um, I can call and see if they have a different room?"

Spencer cleared his throat and seemed to break

from some sort of a trance. "Nah, don't sweat it. We're fake boyfriends, right? One bed makes sense. Wouldn't want Lance to find out we needed to switch to a room with two beds." He crossed the room and tossed his bag onto the desk chair. "We've got this." He flopped onto the bed. "It's nice. And it's pretty big. I promise I won't fake ravage you in your sleep."

Oh God, please, ravage me. I want to be ravaged.

I gulped in some air just as I tried to laugh and ended up choking myself. Rushing to the bathroom, I took a few moments to compose myself.

"You okay?" Spencer asked when I returned.

"Yeah, just needed to use the bathroom."

"Without flushing the toilet or washing your hands?" Spencer cocked a brow.

"Oh, um, yeah. I forgot to use the bathroom," I muttered. "Um, should we go take a look around the place?" I wiped my sweaty palms on my jeans.

Spencer narrowed his eyes at me but nodded and stood from the bed. "Sounds good. Check on rentals, food options, maybe look at the gift shop. There might be something screaming for us to buy it."

I laughed. "I'm not big on souvenirs, but there might be something for Hadley."

We left the room and I did my best to try to forget the fact that not only was I going to be holding hands and possibly kissing Spencer, I was also going to be sharing a bed with him.

Spencer and me in the same bed.

A guy I wanted so badly my eyeballs itched.

Spencer only a few feet away from me while I slept.

Please don't let me do anything stupid like cuddle up to him.

But on second thought, maybe a sleepy cuddle session would be enough to convince Spencer to teach me about sex?

I had a feeling that he'd balk—like hardcore refusal—when I told him I wanted him to help me gain experience with sex. But I also knew that he had a very hard time saying no to me and I was—very selfishly—planning to use that to my advantage.

I just hadn't planned on starting the plan on the ski trip.

But maybe our one bed situation was the perfect opportunity.

Spencer asked the ski shop worker about renting boots and skis. Since a large group was expected, we went ahead and reserved our equipment.

"Want to grab something to eat before we explore around?" Spencer yawned. "I'm not *against* trying to ski today, but I'm honestly tired from the drive.

Maybe we save the risking life and limb part of the trip until tomorrow?"

I laughed. "I honestly just came to be seen and get a checkmark next to my name with the leaders. I'll try skiing, but almost breaking my neck can definitely wait until tomorrow. There seem to be a couple little snack shop type places and a restaurant."

"Let's try the restaurant," Spencer said and headed toward the hotel lobby.

When he reached for my hand, a fluttery buzz traveled through me, my cheeks going warm and my chest filled with a delicious tightness.

"Show time," he whispered in my ear and for a split second I savored his warm closeness, the brush of his lips against my skin.

Until I heard, "There's my boy."

Yanked from the endorphins of Spencer's touch, I jerked my head to find Lance coming our way.

Spencer gave my hand a squeeze. I wasn't even sure what he was trying to tell me, but a feeling of safety and calm washed over me.

"Hey, Lance," I said. "Glad you made it."

My classmate stared at where my hand was slotted perfectly in Spencer's and narrowed his eyes. "Yeah, you too. Didn't know you were bringing a buddy."

"Boyfriend," Spencer said and stepped forward, dropping my hand momentarily. "Spencer Nelson. We met at the game shop." Once Lance had given a halfhearted shake, Spencer moved back to my side and draped his arm over my shoulders. Pulling me close, he kissed the side of my head. "We'll see you around, but Rai and I were just planning to grab some food."

"Join us," Lance said quickly. "Group from school has a table. We're ordering drinks and appetizers. We're going to hit the slopes after."

"I think we're going to hang for today and ski tomorrow," I said.

"Oh, come on. Don't be party poopers. Come drink with us," Lance wheedled.

Spencer tensed next to me. "I don't drink."

I reached up to caress his hand on my shoulder. "Like I said, we're going to get some food and then hang. We'll probably see you out there tomorrow."

Lance sneered. "You don't drink, don't want to hang with friends, going to hole-up in your room instead of ski? Wow, you two are just a barrel of fun." He glanced between Spencer and me as if trying to solve a mystery he didn't quite understand. "Whatever. The rest of us know how to live it up."

"Oh, we'll be having plenty of fun on our own,"

Spencer said with a suggestive smile before brushing a kiss on my cheek. "You ready?"

I nodded, barely able to breathe. "See ya, Lance."

Once we found a table in the restaurant as far away from the school group as possible, Spencer finally let go of me and I collapsed into a chair.

"Do you think we should eat with them so you can be seen by the leaders?" Spencer asked as he handed me a menu.

I stole a glance across the restaurant. "No, those are just students, none of the leaders are in that group. No one to impress. In fact, I figure it will look better that we're having a quiet dinner rather than getting drunk."

Spencer reached for my hand. "You can drink, you know that, right? My decision to avoid alcohol is based on my mom and my past; I don't care if others drink."

I shook my head. "I've tried beer and liquor and wine. I don't love the taste and it usually just makes me sleepy. I'd rather drink water or soda; tastes better and doesn't knock me out."

Spencer nodded his acceptance of my answer. "You did a good job back there. I didn't mean to take you by surprise, but I saw him getting off the elevator and thought it would be good to already be holding your hand when he walked over."

"Yeah, thanks for that. You were great." I smiled and tried not to sigh at the memory of his big, work-roughened hand holding mine. "I don't think he *gets* it, but he definitely noticed we were together."

"I don't know if he doesn't get it or doesn't *like* it, maybe both, but he definitely noticed." Spencer studied the menu. "You want to share? I'll get the burger and split it with you?"

"Oh, that's good because I couldn't decide between the burger and the pizza. Now I can try both." The easy way Spencer and I got along both warmed my heart and made it hurt. I wanted this thing between us to be *real*, not just a show for Lance. Would I *ever* be able to convince Spencer to give us a chance?

He has to love himself before he can love you.

Yeah, well, maybe I could love him enough for both of us while he learns how.

"Perfect. I'm getting fries with ranch, that okay?" Spencer scanned the menu. "And I usually go for well-done at restaurants."

"Works for me. I think I'll get a side of Brussels sprouts."

Spencer wrinkled his nose. "You can keep those."

We placed our orders.

"Oh, come on. You have to at least try them. If

cooked right, they're really good," I said as the wait person walked away.

"One. Only one. That's one thing Bev doesn't like so she doesn't subject me to the evil little green things." Spencer pretended to shiver. "I had them *once* at some church dinner a social worker dragged me to. Mushy, bitter, rock hard centers. So bad."

"No, that's not how they should be. That's why they get such a bad rap. They can't be too big and they have to be cooked right." I bumped his knee with mine. "I promise you'll like them."

"You can still share my fries even when I don't like the Brussels sprouts."

When our food arrived, we spent a few moments splitting the pizza and burger. Spencer put his fries in the middle and I pushed my veggies next to the fries.

"Moment of truth. Try one," I said.

Spencer glared at the plate of green orbs before spearing one with his fork and dipping it in the accompanying sauce. After popping it in his mouth, he chewed, never taking his scowling eyes from mine.

"Fuck," he muttered.

I beamed. "Told you. We need to convince Bev they can be good and get her to cook some."

"Yeah, we really do. If they were cooked like this,

I bet everyone would love them." Spencer popped another sprout into his mouth. "And Bev's a good cook. We just need to get her the right recipe."

We spent the rest of our lunch enjoying the food and company, laughing at stories Cooper or Hadley had told us, and just being together.

"I'll pay the bill," Spencer said as he grabbed the check and headed to the front register.

I pulled out my phone and opened my Venmo. After sending him ten dollars, I watched as he pulled his phone out, checked the notification, shook his head, and flashed me a smile.

When we fell into step beside each other on the way to the elevators, he bumped his elbow into mine. "You know we've paid each other that same ten dollars like five times now."

"I know. I kinda like it. It's kinda our thing."

Spencer's eyes caught mine and he smiled. "Yeah." He cleared his throat. "Want to check the gift shop?"

We spent a bit of time browsing around and picked two books and a cute little snow globe for Hadley.

"Hey, I'll grab these if you'll go check what the sign said about times for the slopes to open and what time the buffet breakfast starts," Spencer suggested.

When we met back at the elevators, I reported the times and Spencer held up the bag for Hadley.

"Nap? Then we can walk around later, see what's going on." I pressed the *Up* button.

"Yes," Spencer said with a yawn. "Don't know why kids hate naps so much. I love them. Not that I get to take many of them, but a good nap makes for a perfect day in my books."

Once to the room, we took our shoes off and took turns in the bathroom.

I changed into lounge pants and Spencer did the same.

Then we climbed into bed and got comfortable. We naturally picked the side of the bed that had us in the same position as our room at home; Spencer to my left, me to his right.

"Sorry if I'm a blanket hog," Spencer said as he curled on his side to face the wall.

"Hopefully I don't toss and turn too much," I said as I tried to calm the pounding in my chest. The bed was bigger than our beds at home, but it felt much smaller once I was *in* it with Spencer so close.

My mind whirled as I lay there, right next to the man who had me all sorts of mixed up inside, and I tried to gather my thoughts.

The way I saw it, I had two options and I needed to make my mind up.

Option one: Stick to the fake boyfriends thing. Kiss and whatnot around Lance, but keep it strictly platonic when it was just Spencer and me.

Option two: Continue the ruse to get Lance off my back, but ask Spencer to do me the huge favor of teaching me about sex.

Option one was safe and easy. It was what we'd planned and was the fair thing to do. But option one would mean going back to being only friends and never getting the chance to experience Spencer the way I wanted.

Option two was risky and had the potential to end a friendship. I shouldn't even have been thinking about it. But the way I looked at it, Spencer and I were close. We were friends already in a situation designed to make it look like we were boyfriends. Why not take advantage of the circumstances and finally put an end to my unwanted celibacy?

Um, maybe because Spencer doesn't like you that way? Maybe because you already asked him to play fake boyfriend? Maybe because you know you won't be able to have sex with him and then go back to being just friends?

My brain logically knew that option two was a terrible idea, but my heart—and my sex starved body —were screaming at me to take the chance.

What could it hurt, really? I was a grown-up. I'd survived on my own after being disowned, surely I could deal with a fake breakup with a fake boyfriend after meaningless sex.

You know damn well it wouldn't be meaningless on your side.

Yeah, but a fun little hookup while already pretending to be boyfriends was the only way I'd ever get to have that with Spencer.

My head basically told me to go fudge myself and refused to keep arguing with my heart, so I settled in under the comfy blankets and let sleep wash over me.

When I woke later, I savored the warmth pressed against my back. Spencer and I were back-to-back in the middle of the bed, warm and cozy under the comforter.

The perfect connection, the delicious heat, blanketed me and I knew I was going to risk it all. Stupid as it maybe was, I couldn't go the safe route this time; I'd regret not taking the chance for the rest of my life.

Maybe Spencer would make it easy for me and refuse.

Maybe he'd laugh in my face and leave my ass at the hotel.

Maybe he'd be so disgusted with my request that he'd demand Bev move me to a different room.

Maybe he'll want a chance at convenient, easy sex and gladly take you up on your offer.

I scoffed and then froze when Spencer stirred.

I wasn't naïve enough to think I'd ask Spencer to have sex with me and he'd just happily agree to it. In fact, I was pretty sure he'd say no. But being friends with Spencer meant knowing him and how to wear him down. I would never ask him to do something he was totally against—fudge that, I respected a person's right to consent and I'd honor Spencer's final decision.

But, there was no getting around it.

I was going to ask Spencer to take advantage of our situation and teach me about sex.

I sighed, glad to have made a decision.

And then I tensed. Just how and when was I going to put this little plan into action?

And what are you going to do when it changes everything you've grown to love about your friendship with Spencer?

I swallowed thickly. Change wasn't always a bad thing, right?

The moment Spencer was awake enough to realize he was plastered against my back, he shifted and pretended to stretch.

The loss of his warm touch made me shiver, but I

played his game and acted as if I was just waking up as well.

"Good nap?" he asked, his voice muffled into the pillow.

"Yeah, you?"

"Mmhm."

"Want to go walk around and see the sites?" I asked. I wasn't going to spring my request on him right then.

"Yeah, sounds good."

We changed back into to our jeans, washed up, and pulled on hoodies before heading out the door.

Midwest Snow was a fairly large resort with three hotels, multiple ski slope options of varying skill levels, several food choices spread around the property, and a small *main street* type stretch filled with shops. During off-season, or when winter snow wasn't enough, the resort made their own snow. Not ideal for elite skiers, but it was good enough for what most folks around the area wanted to do.

We opted to walk the shops, watch some of the skiers, and then grab some food.

As we headed down the street of shops, Spencer took my hand.

I glanced around to see where Lance was.

"I haven't seen him, but better to be ready just in case, right?" Spencer gave my hand a squeeze.

My heart melted. I was so fudged. "Yeah, probably right. You don't mind others seeing you holding my hand?"

Spencer frowned. "Why would I care?" He opened the door to a t-shirt shop.

"People aren't always the friendliest to same-sex couples."

"Nah, doesn't bother me. I haven't done much dating, but that's not because I'm in the closet. The shit I went through in the past keeps me weighted down like a damn lead blanket and the effort it takes to date has always just seemed like too much. But I've never really cared if anyone knew I was gay. Kinda felt like all the other shit of my past was a lot worse than someone not liking me because I like dick." He chuckled as he held up a funny t-shirt. "If you're uncomfortable with it, we can stop." He started to let go of my hand. "Doubt we'll see Lance in the stores anyway."

I gripped his hand and shook my head. "No, it's fine. I don't really care either. After being kicked out by my family, I kinda adopted the attitude that if I could survive my flesh and blood hating me, I could deal with some strangers not liking me. I've never dated, but I think I'd want to be open like this if I found someone who liked me."

"Finding someone to like you won't be a

problem, I can promise you that," Spencer said and then cleared his throat. "You want to get a shirt?"

I blinked away the emotions his words had brought on and shook my head. "Nah, I'm not really the souvenir shirt type."

"Next store?"

We browsed the strip of stores, talking and laughing, holding hands for over an hour. The last store we went into was a toy and game store.

"Ohhh, this is fun. I bet they get a ton of business with families who have kids," I said as I pulled Spencer to a display of game cards.

There was nothing I *had* to have for myself, but the iridescent dice set seemed like something Hadley would like. I held them up and glanced at Spencer.

"For our girl?" he asked with a smirk.

I nodded. "Think she'd like them?"

"Definitely. Especially if we play games with her."

I took the dice to the counter to make my purchase. As I walked out of the store to meet Spencer, my phone buzzed with a notification and I knew he'd sent me ten dollars.

I smiled and let him take my hand as we headed toward the slopes farthest from our hotel. We'd watch the more skilled skiers there and get Mexican for dinner before heading back to our room.

Once we'd seen the slopes—and people who

actually knew what they were doing on skis—we enjoyed dinner before starting back to our place.

As we walked, laughing about how bad we were going to be when we tried to ski the next day, I let my mind believe, just for a moment, that the evening with Spencer had been a real date.

"Oh look, my favorite guy," Lance's voice sounded from behind me and I instantly squeezed Spencer's hand—my imagination wilting as I remembered the whole reason Spencer was even with me, let alone holding my hand.

Later, I could broach the subject of sex with Spencer. For the time being, I needed to make sure Lance knew I wasn't available or interested.

"Hey, man," Spencer gave a brief nod as we paused to speak to Lance.

Lance shot a disinterested look toward Spencer before eyeing me up and down. "Raiden, we're going to swim and hit the hot tub, work out some of the kinks from the slopes. I'll save you a spot next to me in the sauna," he gave a wink that I guessed was supposed to be sexy, but it only made me feel dirty.

"We've got plans," Spencer growled, dropping my hand and wrapping an arm around me so I was in front of him, protected by his touch across my chest.

"Can Raiden speak for himself?" Lance sneered.

Spencer leaned in to press kisses against my neck and whispered, "Go ahead, speak for yourself."

For show or not, there was nowhere I wanted to be but with Spencer. Breathless from the heat coursing through me at Spencer's touch, I smiled and told Lance, "We definitely have plans."

As Lance narrowed his eyes, Spencer nuzzled my neck and gave me a boost of confidence for what I said next. "Lance, I'm with Spencer. He's my boyfriend and I love him very much."

Not a lie. But even though Spencer thought I was just putting on a show, his arm tensed around me. Too much? Tough. I needed Lance to get a damn clue.

"Well, enjoy your night. You know where to find me when he dumps your ass and you need a new dick to worship." Lance grinned, not in a friendly way, and adjusted the front of his pants. "I'll give you what you want."

Spencer moved quickly and stepped in front of me. He was taller than me which put him several inches taller than Lance and it gave me a little thrill to see Lance flinch back as Spencer moved into his space.

"Listen, asshole," Spencer bit out. "Whether he's with someone or not, he's not interested. He's said no, he means no. Stop with the come-ons and harassment. It's not a good look for you."

I stepped beside Spencer and curled my arm through his.

Lance just scoffed. "Whatever. I don't know what the two of you see in each other, but have at it. I'll be waiting." He curled his lip and gave us a disgusted look before turning to pop into a store.

Spencer huffed and we turned toward the hotel.

As he took my hand again—and I had to keep telling myself it was all for show—he grumbled, "Damn, that guy can't take a hint, huh?"

"Yeah, he's persistent. I don't wish him on anyone, but I need him to find someone else to fixate on." I pointed toward a food truck. "Let's get pretzels for dessert."

"Perfect," Spencer said with a smile and a kiss on my cheek. But he pulled back quickly. "Sorry, got into the show back there and kinda forgot myself."

I was sure he could feel the heat from my cheeks, hear the pounding of my heart. "No problem, never going to turn down your kisses," I murmured.

Spencer stared at me for a moment and then cleared his throat. "So, pretzels?"

By the time we arrived at the hotel—four pretzels in a bag, two for dessert and two for a snack the next day—I was dragging.

"Can we shower and just relax with a mindless movie or something?" I asked.

"I'm down. Early night may help us on the skis tomorrow." Spencer raised his brow as he made his suggestion and then we both laughed. "Okay, okay. Nothing is going to help us on the skis tomorrow. But at least we'll be well-rested for busting our asses."

A bit later, finished with our showers, full of pretzels, and dressed in lounge pants and shirts, we pulled down the comforter.

"You care if I sleep in my boxers like at home?" Spencer asked, a guilty look on his face.

"What?" My brows came together. "No, of course not. Sleep however you're most comfortable." *Oh, holy fudge, I was going to be in bed with Spencer in only his underwear.* "You know I'm a tank and boxers guy. We should both just do our normal thing." I shucked my lounge pants and climbed into bed, telling myself I could *not* watch as Spencer stripped to his boxers.

But I couldn't help it. He'd turned to face the covered window as he pulled his shirt over his head, revealing a strong back and trim waist. When he pushed his pants down to uncover two of the most delicious-looking dimples right above the elastic of his boxer briefs, I nearly swallowed my tongue.

As Spencer turned toward the bed, I jerked my

head back to the television screen and tried to pretend I wasn't about to jizz myself like a fudging teen because I'd caught a glimpse of his bulge under the cotton material.

Holy shit. What if Spencer agreed to teach me about sex? Could I even do it? No, no I couldn't. I'd end up a quivering, awkward mess who would probably blow his load the first time I even saw Spencer's dick for real.

Damnit. Now, I was hard.

Perfect. A boner in bed with my best friend slash fake boyfriend.

I yanked a spare pillow over my lap and tried to focus on the movie.

"It's early, but I swear I could sleep already," Spencer yawned and turned off the bedside lamp.

"Yeah, same," I muttered. Should I ask about sex? Go ahead and just get it over with? I wanted him so badly, but I was also scared to death he'd say no. No, that wasn't right. I expected him to say no—at least at first—but I think I was the most afraid of him being angry or ending our friendship.

If you really *thought he was going to end your friendship, you wouldn't be considering the sex request. You're not the type to throw away a friend like Spencer for something you've lived just fine without for twenty-five years.*

I sighed.

Okay, maybe I was more worried about being embarrassed to bring up sex.

I knew in my heart that Spencer wasn't the type to end our friendship over my awkward, fumbling ridiculousness about sex.

He'd tell me no. He'd tell me I deserved better. He'd tell me that he wasn't worth sharing that part of me with.

And I'd just have to tell him the truth. Spencer was the *only* person in my entire life who I trusted enough to share that with.

Mind made up, I turned toward Spencer.

And found him sound asleep, soft snores escaping his perfect lips.

EIGHT
SPENCER

Holy fuck.

I was in *way* over my head with no idea how to get out alive.

I liked holding Rai's hand and kissing him *a lot* more than I'd been prepared for.

Waking up plastered against him after our nap? I had to fight the urge to roll over, pull him into my arms, and kiss him senseless.

The entire day had felt like an easy, comfortable date with a man I was head-over-heels for. Everything with Rai was so damn easy and it was simple to forget we were faking the whole thing.

Damn Lance.

I mean, I guess I should have been thanking the guy because without his slimy-ass harassment and inability to take no for an answer, Rai would have had no reason to ask me to be his fake boyfriend.

But I couldn't give any appreciation to Lance because he was scum.

However, I could totally appreciate Rai's long, lean body as he stripped down to his boxer briefs, and the way the snug tank hugged his torso. I could have stared at him all damn day.

Instead, I begged out of more interaction by claiming I was tired. In truth, I was. I hadn't done much physically, but maybe the mental and emotional stress of hiding my feelings for Rai had started to take a toll.

Closing my eyes and willing sleep to come, I blocked out the movie and the warmth of Rai so close to me—mere inches away—I could have reached out and touched him so easily.

I swallowed hard and breathed slowly until sleep won out.

When I woke—groggy and slightly disoriented, I could tell it wasn't morning yet—I snuggled close to Rai and pressed my lips against the back of his neck.

Oh, fuck.

I froze and assessed my situation. My big spoon was curled around Rai's perfect little spoon, my arm draped over his ribcage, my hand holding his.

How in the actual fuck did we end up cuddled together?

And a better question was how in the hell did I extricate myself without waking Rai. If he woke, it would alert him to the fact that his best friend and fake boyfriend would rather skip his next breath than let go of him—not to mention, the rock-hard cock pressing against his ass would likely cause some confusion and need for explaining.

Which I couldn't do.

I couldn't explain how I'd gone and fallen so hard for him.

I couldn't explain how being around him made me feel whole for the first time in my entire life.

I couldn't explain how I dreaded the day Lance moved on because it would mean we could go back to being just friends.

Slowly, and as gently as possible, I tried to slip my hand from Rai's so I could roll away from him.

But his breathy moan and squeeze of my hand gave me pause.

"Stay," Rai whispered.

"I'm *really* sorry about this. Didn't realize I was a cuddler. Never had anyone in my bed so this is new for me," I babbled. I needed to bolt from the bed. Needed to take a cold shower. Needed to stop breathing in Rai's apricot facewash and coconut shampoo.

"I like it," Rai answered quietly, his thumb

caressing my hand. "Can I ask you something? And you know you can say no—and I figure you will because this is a *huge* ask."

Involuntarily, my arm tightened around his chest. "What? Is something wrong?"

Rai shifted and rolled to face me. "You know I'm a virgin, right?"

Unable to breathe, I blinked slowly. I might have nodded. Lack of oxygen to my brain was making things fuzzy.

"And you know you're my best friend and the one person I trust most in this world, right?"

Again, an oxygen-deprived blink and nod. With no air reaching my lungs and all the blood pooled in my dick, I figured I had less than a minute before I expired right there in the bed.

Rai's eyes were on mine and, in the dim light from the bathroom, he bit his lip. "I want you to teach me about sex," he said.

Clearly, I'd died and already ascended to the pearly gates because what I *thought* I'd heard my sexy-as-hell best friend and fake boyfriend say was that he wanted me to teach him about sex.

"Spencer? Did you hear me?" Rai's hand cupped my face.

I think I may have grunted some sort of reply.

"I want to learn, want to practice, and you're the

only person in my life who I'd trust with something this big," Rai said in a rush. "I know you won't judge or push me."

My mind continued to short-circuit, attempting to race a million miles a minute while also shutting down. I had no coherent thoughts, no words.

"Spencer? You're kinda freaking me out. Can you say something?"

I started and stopped multiple times before I finally formed the first words my brain could string together. "Probably a bad idea."

Rai's entire body sagged against me and I immediately felt like a heel for telling him no.

Sometimes telling people no is for their own good. Sometimes telling people no is for your sanity.

But sometimes, telling people no is simply to save you from a new and overwhelmingly scary situation.

"Hear me out, please?" Rai whispered.

I nodded, pressing a kiss against his forehead.

"I want to date and fall in love. But I have zero idea of what I'm doing in the bedroom—aside from porn, which I realize isn't the best teacher—and I want to know more and have more confidence." Rai curled into my chest, our joined hands captured between us. "I don't want to practice with hookups…"

*Good. Fuck if I could deal with Rai hooking up with
random dudes just to learn about sex.*

"And I don't want to go into a relationship with
someone just to learn about sex," he continued.
"Since we're doing this whole fake thing, I thought
maybe you could teach me."

My brain had finally caught up—at least
somewhat—and I cleared my throat. "What are you
wanting to learn?" Maybe if he just needed some
things explained and a few technique pointers—and
let's face it, I wasn't exactly the most experienced, so
who was I to give tips?—I could probably help at
least a bit.

"Everything," Rai answered. "I want it all. I want
to learn how to do things and experience what it's
like to have those things done to me." The warmth
of his breath against my chest sent goosebumps
across my skin. "I want to know what it's like to do
it all; find out what I like, figure out how to make
someone else feel good."

The lack of oxygen was back and I'd probably
black out soon. I should have said no right then and
there. It was a terrible idea and I knew I wouldn't
survive sex with Rai and then slotting him back into
the friend category. How in the ever-loving fuck was
I supposed to have Rai in my bed and then watch

him take all we'd shared together into his first *real* relationship?

Yet, my body was at war. My head said it was stupid and I needed to run far, far away from anything resembling sex with Rai. My cock argued that the circumstances were perfect for a little fucking around and urged me to take advantage of Rai's request.

My heart? My heart was the one I worried about the most. I'd fallen hard for Rai. Did I want to have sex with him? Hell, yes. Could my heart handle being that close to him and then letting him go?

The way my chest was already aching, I had a feeling that the answer was a resounding *no*, I definitely wouldn't survive it.

"I still think it's a terrible idea. Too many risks and too much chance of someone getting hurt," I grumbled.

"I get it," Rai answered softly. "I knew it was too much to ask and I'd never put you in a situation where you had to do something you didn't want to do." He shrugged against me. "I just can't imagine trusting anyone else enough to teach me."

"It's not because I don't want to." I closed my eyes against the onslaught of thoughts and feelings rushing through me. "Sex changes things," I started.

"Yeah," Rai whispered. "But if we know it's just a learning experience and it ends when the whole fake boyfriends thing ends, maybe we can keep the changes minimal? You're my best friend and I trust you to keep me safe and take care of me. We always have fun together…what's the harm in adding a little bit more?"

The harm is that I'll be left with nothing but memories and a broken heart when it all comes crashing down.

I took a deep breath. I was going to regret the decision, I knew I would. But if I turned down the request—knowing that Rai would eventually end up learning in the arms of some other guy—it would haunt me for the rest of my life.

Either way, I was facing heartache.

Might as well take what Rai was offering because a *real*, intimate relationship with him would never be on the table.

"We start slow," I offered.

Rai's body thrummed to life in my arms. "For real?" He lifted his head, eyes meeting mine.

"*Slow*," I reiterated.

"Can we start now?" Rai whispered.

Fuck.

I was done for. There was no way I was making it out of this alive.

Make the most of it and enjoy it while it lasts.

Cupping Rai's face, I leaned in to brush a

kiss over his lips, but the contact sparked a heated current between us and I was helpless to stop. Rai moaned against my mouth and that was all it took. Growling, I deepened the kiss, wrapping Rai tightly in my arms and teasing with my tongue until he whimpered and opened for me.

Allowing myself to forget the fake part, I dove into the kiss and savored Rai's flavor, every whimper and moan, and the slick glide of our tongues. My hand caressed down his back, snaking under his shirt to find soft, warm skin.

Rai rocked his hips, silently seeking more. My hand moved to cup his ass and pull him flush against me, our rock-hard cocks brushing together, separated only by the thin material of our boxers.

"Can we get naked?" Rai panted. "Want to feel you against me."

"Naked isn't slow," I said, but I was already working his shirt over his head and yanking off my underwear.

He scrambled to remove his boxers and soon we were plastered back together, hot skin, roaming hands, wet kisses, and hard cocks in a writhing mess of movement. I wanted to pause time, to catalog every part of his body, every heated point of contact between us.

"I could come like this," Rai said, sounding somewhat embarrassed and a little bit in awe.

"Roll over, put your back against me," I ordered as I stretched to reach the towel I'd left on the floor. With Rai's back pressed to my front, and my cock nearly bursting because of Rai's ass rocking into me, I spread the towel out on the bed in front of Rai. "Save you from the wet spot," I murmured against his ear.

Rai chuckled. "Such a gentleman."

The comment went straight to my gut. "Not feeling very gentlemanly right now."

"How are you feeling?"

"Like I'm an asshole who's about to take advantage of his best friend," I muttered.

"I feel the same." Rai pushed his ass against me. "But if we're both assholes taking advantage of our best friend, maybe it cancels out." He reached for my arm and pulled it over his torso. "Please, show me. Give me this." Rai turned his head, his lips so close. "I wanna feel it, wanna come apart in your arms." He captured my mouth with his and kissed me, warm lips and slow tongues becoming one.

I continued the kiss as my fingers glided over his neck, toyed with his nipples and trailed lower to brush against the soft skin of his abdomen. "What do you want?" I asked breathlessly when the kiss broke apart.

"Touch me. Wanna feel your hand on me," Rai begged.

I teased the thatch of hair at the base of his cock, loving Rai's quick intake of breath, before moving to cup his balls. Fuck, it had been a while since I'd been with anyone—like, a *long* while—and I'd never been in a situation where I could take my time and enjoy my partner. Hell, I'd never *wanted* to take my time with anyone else. But with Rai, I wanted to savor each and every touch, bask in his little grunts and groans, draw out any bit of time we had together.

My own leaking cock, pressed snuggly against Rai's ass, was arguing for hard and fast, but I willed the sentiment away and teased a finger against the silky skin under Rai's balls.

"Oh, shit, that's good. Feeling someone else's fingers there is amazing," Rai panted.

My imagination had a heyday picturing Rai touching himself and I shifted my hand to stroke the underside of his hard cock. Reaching the swollen, leaking head, I thumbed through the pre-cum as I teased his slit. I wanted to roll him over and take him in my mouth, but I'd said slow.

"You're killing me, Spence. Can you please just touch me?"

I chuckled. "I *am* touching you."

He grunted. "You know what I mean. Put your hand around me, jerk me." He gasped when I pressed an open-mouth kiss against his neck. "Please."

"Like this," I whispered at his ear as I took his length in my hand and stroked.

"Oh, shit. Fudge. Holy shit, yeah," Rai babbled.

"You're a noisy little thing, you know that?" I teased, stroking slowly.

"Sorry." Rai thrust into my fist. "Can't help it. Feels too good."

"Don't ever be sorry. Love hearing you."

"I wanna come. I'm close." Rai reached behind, his hand gripping my hip.

"Not too far myself. You okay with me shooting on your ass like this?" I pressed my cock against him.

"Oh, God, yeah," Rai panted. "So good."

As I stroked him, gathering the slick of his pre-cum and increasing my pressure and speed, I whispered, "Talk to me. Tell me what you want to learn."

Rai groaned. "Want it all. Wanna see you over me, coming on my stomach. Wanna feel your hot mouth on me. Drop to my knees and suck you, taste your cum."

Holy shit, asking him to talk was going to be what sent me over the damn edge. "Yeah, wanna taste you, too. What else?"

Rai's thrusting hips increased their speed and a little moan escaped his lips. "Wanna lick your ass and learn how to get you off. Wanna feel your tongue on me, your fingers in me. Feel that stretch, need the burn. God, I want your cock in me. Gotta feel it."

Fuck.

I was a goner. "Yeah, fuck, yeah. God, that sounds so good."

"Spence, I'm going to come," Rai whined. "Please, wanna come so bad."

"Do it, come for me." I stroked faster, twisting my fist as I reached his swollen head. My own balls drew up tight, cock ready to explode, but I wanted his release first.

Rai's body tensed and he whimpered, his hand on my hip gripping tightly as he pulled me hard against him. A low moan sounded deep in his chest as his cock pulsed in my hand, his load shooting onto the towel and dripping over my fingers.

He sagged against me as he came down from his high. "Can't decide if I want to turn over and jack you off or have you come all over my ass just like this."

"Shit, Rai," I growled between gritted teeth. "Talk

like that and it won't matter because I'll blow my load before you make up your mind."

He chuckled, sounding sated and sleepy. "Wanna do it all, but can't move. Come on my ass."

I groaned and brought my cum-slick hand to my own cock and began to stroke.

As if I needed any encouragement, Rai turned over his shoulder to kiss me. "Next time, I want to touch. Want to spread my legs for you and watch our cocks rub together until we're both covered in cum."

That image, and my tight fist, was all it took before I was unloading on Rai's gorgeous ass. With my forehead pressed against his shoulder and my dick still throbbing in my hand, I watched in the shadowy glow of the bathroom light as my release ran across his skin and knew I'd never be the same. His kiss, his touch, his damn words had ruined me for anyone else.

Our time together wasn't even over and my heart was already broken.

I'd never recover from having this and losing it.

"Was that okay?" Rai whispered.

"Amazing," I said and pressed a kiss against his shoulder. "We should clean up and sleep."

I wiped Rai's back with the towel and we took turns washing our hands.

"Can we try sleeping naked? I've never done that." Rai asked as we left the bathroom.

I laughed. "Sure. Can't say I do it often, too many housemates and don't want to give anyone a sight they'd rather not see."

After crawling into bed naked, Rai cuddled against my chest, we were silent for several moments, just our breathing and the hum of the room filling the air.

"Thank you," Rai whispered. "I know it's not real, and that's okay. But I can't imagine opening myself to someone else like that. Thank you for giving this to me."

I kissed the top of his head, desperate to scream that what I felt for him *was* real—so very real—but closing my eyes against the pain. "You're welcome. Thank you for trusting me." In the perfect world, I'd be the type of man Rai deserved and we could ride off happily into the sunset.

This was not a perfect world.

Just when I thought Rai was drifting to sleep, he looked up and kissed me. "Can we have another lesson in the morning?"

I laughed and kissed him back. "We'll see."

Yeah, this was going to fucking kill me.

WHEN I AWOKE, Rai in my arms, warm and cozy, I waited for the awkwardness and regret to fill me, but it never came.

I replayed the night before with Rai, sending my cock way past the morning wood phase. Giving Rai his first orgasm in the arms of someone he trusted, someone who loved him—even if that little tidbit had to remain under lock and key—meant everything to me. I had no regrets about what we'd done and looked forward to teaching Rai more.

My only regret was knowing he didn't feel for me what I felt for him and this little arrangement would eventually come to a screeching halt.

Trying not to think about what it would be like to go from sex with Rai back to just two friends sharing a room—hell, maybe even having to watch Rai start dating and bringing guys home—I opted to play ostrich. Head in the sand and ignoring reality. I'd just enjoy giving Rai what he wanted and deal with the fallout later.

"Is this the awkward morning after where all our good senses come flooding back and we realize with major regret what a huge mistake we made?" Rai whispered as he snuggled deeper into my embrace.

"No regrets here," I murmured against his ear. "Unless you count the regret of actually having to get out of bed at some point today."

"I've heard skiing is overrated," Rai quipped. "Maybe bed all day is the best bet."

I chuckled softly against his neck, loving his scent and pressing kisses along the soft skin. "Nah, there's a breakfast downstairs. Plus, you need to be seen by your group leaders *and* we need to be sure Lance sees us."

Rai sighed and sagged against me. "Yeah, I guess." He seemed disappointed. He was quiet for a moment before speaking again. "Can we mess around before we get up?"

"I like the way you think," I answered. "Can we pause long enough for a quick piss?"

"Only if we add in enough time for brushing our teeth. Pretty sure dragon breath is decidedly unsexy."

"First one back in bed gets to choose how we get off?" I suggested, knowing I'd purposely let Rai get back in bed first because my new favorite pastime was getting him off.

"Deal." Rai scrambled from the bed, his feet tangling in his jeans on the floor as he bumped into the wall.

"Damn, man. Don't hurt yourself before the fun even starts."

"Just wait until you see me on the slopes," Rai quipped.

Laughing, we rushed to the bathroom—which was like most hotels with the sink outside of where the shower and toilet were housed—and took turns using the bathroom and brushing our teeth.

We raced back to the bed and I only slowed enough to be sure Rai landed on the mattress first before I followed him down and gathered him in my arms.

"Hi," Rai whispered after a long, slow good morning kiss.

I smiled. "Hi."

"I thought waking up naked in bed with my best friend after asking him to teach me about sex and having his cum all over my ass would be awkward," Rai rushed out.

"And?" I cocked a brow and smirked at his words.

He shook his head, eyes full of mischief and wonder. "It's not. And I have you to thank for that. You could have made me feel bad for asking, feel weird for needing this level of trust, but you didn't. You did what you do best and gave me exactly what I needed." Rai leaned in and kissed me, a deep, exploring kiss that had my dick stirring back to life. "Thank you. For this, for being my friend, just for everything."

See, he's keeping it friend zoned. Maybe friends with

temporary benefits, but still just friends. Don't let that out of your head. Don't go doing something stupid.

Too late.

Rai was seared in my head, coursing through my blood, imprinted on my heart.

But I pushed it all away and smiled. "Not like it's a hardship for me. Spend time with my best friend, take some trips, eat some dinners, *and* get great sex while hopefully pissing off and sending a douchebag on his way? What's not to enjoy?"

Rai snorted. "*Great* sex? Pretty sure my fumbling and learning doesn't exactly qualify."

"Disagree." I rolled him onto his back, savoring the way his long, lean legs opened for me, and settled between his spread thighs. "Last night was some of the best sex I've ever had. I told you, my experience with sex hasn't been a super positive one. One woman who helped confirm without a shadow of a doubt that I was gay and several meaningless, hard and fast hookups with strangers don't exactly lend themselves to a great sex life." I leaned down and pressed kisses against his collarbone. "I'm probably the least qualified to *teach* you anything about sex."

"What you lack in positive sex experiences, you make up for in the way I trust you and the way you protect me. No one else I want these firsts with and I just need you to know I appreciate you. Not many friendships could withstand this."

I snorted.

"What?"

"Just thinking how Cooper and I could *never* do this. The thought of touching his dick or kissing him? Nope. I guess there are different types of friendships." My shoulders shook with laughter as I imagined Cooper and I trying to get each other off.

Dumbass, that's because you love Cooper as a friend and you're not attracted to him. You've fallen in love with Rai and you're crazy about him as more than just a friend.

The thought sobered me and I changed the subject. "I believe you said something about getting off?" I waggled my brow.

Rai wrapped his arms around my neck and pulled me in for a deep, seeking kiss. "Can we rub off like this?" Rocking his hips up, he pressed his hard cock against mine.

The delicious friction sent sparks through me and I groaned. "If it means your cock against mine and watching you come? Definitely, yes."

Rai smiled and continued rocking his hips. "Tell me about the things you'll show me, things you'll do to me," he begged.

I snaked my arms under his shoulders, putting us chest-to-chest as I set a steady rhythm of thrusting. Between imagining all the things I wanted to do to Rai and the delicious hot slide of our cocks, I knew getting off wasn't going to take long. "Wanna suck you off, tongue your ass. Wanna see you on your knees, your mouth full of my cock."

Rai whimpered. "Damn, Spence. Love when you talk like that. Wanna taste you, your cock and your ass. Wanna feel you inside me," he panted. "Shit, shit, shit, I'm gonna come." With his fingers digging into my ass, his legs tangled around mine, and his face buried in my neck, Rai writhed beneath me, rubbing our cocks hard and fast.

"Go ahead, come," I said. "Wanna see you, feel your hot cum on my cock."

The words sent him over and Rai's body tensed in my arms as his release coated our cocks and his stomach.

Pushing up on my arms, I savored the view of his spent cock soaked in his cum. "Look at us, Rai. Watch me come on you," I ordered and thrust hard against him. My orgasm washed over me and I growled as my cock pulsed ropes of hot cum onto Rai's stomach.

Never having the opportunity to enjoy the *after* part of sex before, I dropped to my elbows and pulled Rai in for a long, slow kiss as I enjoyed the slick, wet heat of our mixed cum pressed between our stomachs.

"Fuuuudge," Rai moaned when we finally broke the kiss. "I want to try everything, but *that* will always be a go-to. That was so hot."

His words reminding me that I was just a friend acting as instructor, I smiled and gave him a smacking kiss. "Never gonna hear me complain. Now, let's shower and get this day started."

We ended up in the shower together, but it was just a quick wash and rinse before we dressed and headed to breakfast.

"If we're not too sore tonight, lessons can continue?" Rai asked as he took my hand.

Right as my heart began to soar at the touch, I noticed Lance and some of Rai's classmates standing in line for the buffet. I gave his hand a squeeze. "Yeah, sure."

Skiing turned out to be fairly fun—maybe not an activity I'd *choose* for the next weekend outing I took, but not as terrible as I'd been expecting. We stuck to the bunny slope for a while and only dared the smallest of all the hills once we were feeling a little confident.

One thing about skiing I wasn't prepared for was how quickly the time went when sailing down the hill, but how much time was spent waiting in line for the lift, riding back to the top, and waiting for the crowd to thin out so you weren't tangling and crashing down the hill on your next turn. Maybe that last part was just me not liking to be packed together on the hill.

While we waited in line for hot chocolate, Rai tensed next to me as he took hold of my arm.

"There's my boy," Lance cooed as he sauntered up to us in his snow gear, skis in hand. "You ready for a lesson? I can take you for a ride on the big boy slope."

I wanted to intervene, but also knew Rai was completely capable and needed to do this for himself. "No. I'm good. My *boyfriend* and I are taking a few more trips down the hill and then calling it a day." He leaned in and pressed a kiss against my cheek— sure, all for show, but it made me shiver all the same. "We're going to enjoy the warm shower, comfy bed, and room service for the rest of our time here. Have fun and be careful." Rai pulled on my arm so we could step up in line and left Lance behind.

I glanced over my shoulder, gave a wicked grin and wink to the douche, and then brushed a kiss against Rai's head before quietly saying, "Good job. That was hot."

Rai smiled and shrugged. "It's easier when you're by my side," he whispered.

"Hey, um, you need a plus one to the cohort dinner?" Lance asked as he stepped up beside us in line *again*.

"No," Rai said forcefully. "I'll be there with Spencer."

A girl behind us scoffed. "Dude, I've just watched your pathetic ass get denied twice in less than five minutes. Get a clue."

Lance sneered while Rai and I both chuckled.

"Go on," the girl gestured. "Take that sad game elsewhere."

Lance mumbled something unbecoming about people sticking their noses where they didn't belong, but he whipped around and stalked away.

Rai turned around and smiled at the girl. "Thanks. He doesn't get it."

"Ugh, so annoying. I mean, it's sad really, having to watch that level of awkward come-ons and denials play out—but kinda enjoyable to see guys like him taken down a few notches. Sorry if I was pushy. I just couldn't stand here waiting on my hot drink and watch that pathetic show any longer." She grimaced and pretended to shiver. "Yuck. Nah, that man needed to move along."

"You're fine. Maybe the more he hears it from me and others, he'll finally get the idea." Rai gave her another smile and turned back to move our place up in line.

With our hot chocolate in hand, we took a break at the patio area. "So, I was serious with what I told him," Rai started before taking a sip. "I want a couple more times down the hill—praying each won't be the one where I concuss myself or break a bone—then I want a hot shower and room service in bed with my fake boyfriend."

I smiled, wishing like hell the *fake* could have been removed. "Sounds good. Only thing I'd change?"

Rai cocked a brow.

"Use that big ol' spa tub instead of the shower. Can't do much sexy shit in the public hot tub, but the bathtub in our room has the jets and we could see about bubble bath in the gift shop." With my cheeks hot against the cold air, I tried to sound nonchalant, but the idea of soaking in a warm, bubbly bath with Rai was one I knew would fuel my memories for years to come after we went back to our status quo.

Rai bit his lip. "If this damn hot chocolate wasn't nearly scalding hot still, I'd chug it, race down the hill, and pretty much sprint to the room to get that idea started."

I laughed. "No burning your mouth, I have plans for it later."

Rai's eyes caught fire and he licked his lips as he wedged his knee between my legs. "You don't play fair. How am I supposed to concentrate going down the hill and not crash when all I can think about is sucking your cock?" He shook his head. "Fudge, Spence. That's just cruel."

"If it helps, I'll be having the same difficulties while I think about sucking *your* cock," I said before taking a sip and smiling at him over my paper coffee cup.

Rai stood up and tossed his still steaming drink into the trashcan. "No, it doesn't *help*." He reached for my hand. "Come on. We need to get down this hill, stat."

I laughed and threw away my own cup. "Such a waste of hot chocolate," I teased.

"We can order some from room service."

We ended up enjoying three more times down the hill—amazing what the adrenaline of making it down alive could convince a person to do—before returning our gear.

"You can keep it until tomorrow," the person behind the counter at the equipment rental told us. "You've got the gear until four o'clock."

"Nah, we're probably leaving before that. Gonna

call it quits while we're ahead," Rai said with a smile before we grabbed our shoes from the locker we'd rented.

"There's a microwave in the room, right?" I asked as we started toward the hotel.

"Yeah, why?"

"Let's get food and take it back. Cheaper than room service and probably better."

Rai agreed and we ended up getting a pizza, Chinese noodles, and four burritos.

"Pretty sure this is *not* cheaper than room service," he joked as we stopped by a cupcake truck.

I laughed. "Yeah, but it makes me think of what it would have been like to live on campus for college. Lots of junk food and just relaxing in the room." I pointed toward the menu. "I'm getting the peanut butter chocolate one. What do you want?"

"Mmm, the wedding cake. Always white cake and white icing," Rai said as he took the carry-out boxes from my hands and stepped to the side.

While waiting in the thankfully short line, my phone buzzed. Pulling it out, I saw ten dollars from Rai and couldn't help but laugh as I shot him a look. I knew it was silly and it was just ten dollars, but the fact that we kinda had our own little private joke with the money back and forth warmed my heart.

Once we had our cupcakes, we headed to the

hotel. I pointed to the gift shop as we neared the elevators. "Let me check on the bubble bath."

"Okay, I'll go on up and get dinner ready," Rai said.

It was the type of moment where I wanted to kiss him before sending him on his way, but Lance wasn't around and there was really no reason other than *wanting* to kiss him, so I gave a quick nod and let him go.

While I was browsing the gift shop—which was more a gift shop plus convenience store type combo —I noticed a tiny, very limited display of condoms and lube.

Fuck.

I licked my lips. Buying them would mean we were prepared if that's what Rai wanted. But moving to anal would *not* be on my list of *going slow* activities.

I forced myself to move away from the items and grab the small bottle of children's bubble bath before stalking to the counter to pay.

As I rode the elevator up to the room, I thought about the condoms. Rai had indicated he wanted anal sex. Even if he'd never been sexually active and I'd never had anything but negative results—and no sexual partners since my last *two* tests—I knew I needed to pound it into Rai's head that condoms were a must. I couldn't let him think it was okay with me and then have him lax when it came to other partners.

Maybe if things were real between us, maybe if we weren't planning to go back to friends, we could discuss it. But I couldn't chance it.

Rai is a grown man. He knows about safety—hell, he's in the medical field. Pretty sure he can decide if one situation is safe and another isn't.

I shook my head. Didn't matter. As the person teaching him and protecting him, I needed to be sure we took precautions.

And not having the condoms and lube with us that weekend would end up being a blessing in disguise because it forced us to stick to the *go-slow* plan.

When I reached the room, Rai's smile nearly knocked me over when I walked through the door. Maybe I couldn't get the romantic relationship for real, but I'd be crazy to walk away from the friendship; no matter how badly it hurt, I *had* to keep Rai in my life when this was all over.

"Dinner is served," Rai said as he swept his arm toward the desk where he'd spread the food out and provided forks. He sat in the desk chair and patted the seat of the other chair. "Come on, let's eat before it gets cold."

"Okay, but cupcakes later; I'm going to be stuffed." I sat down and we settled into a comfortable silence while we enjoyed the pizza, noodles, and burritos.

"I kinda never want to go back," Rai commented. "It's been really nice being away. Like, I love my life and moving into Remington Place has been such a blessing, but stepping away from the job and classes has been good."

I chewed my pizza. "I get that. Kinda like a break I didn't realize I needed. Never thought to take time off—what was the point? Go on a trip by myself? Hang out in my room? But being here has shown me that taking a breather isn't a bad thing."

"Even when you're rid of your fake boyfriend, we should plan trips."

I raised my brows.

"What?" Rai shrugged. "Friends take trips, right? We can ask Jesse and Cooper to come along."

"Yeah, maybe." I didn't want to commit to a trip where I wasn't allowed to kiss Rai or hold him in my arms.

Dumbass, you're committing to that by keeping your mouth shut and not telling him how you really feel.

"So, are you a bottom or a top?" Rai asked around a mouth of noodles.

I nearly choked on the burrito I was swallowing.

"Sorry, just figured we could enjoy our meal while I awkwardly ask really personal questions," Rai deadpanned.

Laughing, I cleared my throat. "Um, I mostly top. I'm not *against* bottoming. Just when I think of sex, I'm usually topping."

Rai let loose a breath. "Yeah, I guess when I'm imagining sex, I usually see myself bottoming. Not saying I wouldn't give topping a try, with the right person." He shrugged. "What can you tell me about prep? I mean, I've read some stuff and I'll buy some enemas and whatnot."

I couldn't believe I was having this conversation. A few months ago, I'd been offering a near stranger a roll from my dinner plate at the diner and now I was having sex with my best friend and fielding his questions about prep for anal sex. I took a deep breath and blew it out slowly. "I think a lot of it is just what feels right and works for the person doing the prep. Some like to rely on a good diet and lots of fiber, or just timing sex right. Some like to do a thorough prep with enemas and similar. I'm sure there are about a hundred other options. No matter what, good hygiene is a must. So, you'll just have to decide what works for you."

Rai nodded. "Yeah, that makes sense."

"You ready for that bubble bath?" I asked as we closed up our leftovers.

"Mmhm," Rai hummed. "I know we're taking it slow, but I was hoping maybe blow jobs before the end of the night."

Nearly swallowing my tongue, I chuckled. "Yeah, that can probably be arranged. Come on, let's get the tub filled."

Ten minutes later, I had a warm, slippery, wet Rai between my legs, his back pressed against my front. Bubbles surrounded us and the relaxing jets of the spa tub massaged the sore muscles from the day on the slopes.

"This is nice," Rai murmured.

I kissed the side of his neck before tugging on his chin and bringing his mouth to mine. Biting at his bottom lip, I slid my tongue against the soft skin and waited for Rai to open for me. As I played with his nipple, Rai whimpered, inviting my probing tongue to mate with his. My hand moved down his slick torso, tickling lightly at his smooth abdomen, before taking his plump cock in my fist. After a few strokes and Rai's mouth devouring mine, I moved my other hand to cup his balls.

Rai gasped and turned quickly in my arms, sloshing water over the edge of the tub. "Don't know how you get me so close, so fast," he whispered against my mouth as he straddled me and rocked his cock against mine. "But I'm right there and I want to come."

"What about blow jobs," I teased against his lips even as I reached between us to grasp our hard cocks.

"Later. Want this right now." Rai rocked on my lap, writhing and whimpering as I stroked our cocks and teased his nipples with my teeth and tongue.

Within moments, the thrusting and stroking turned frantic as Rai's head fell back, the muscles in his neck stretched while he moaned. I continued jacking our cocks, sliding my thumb over our slits, as I licked and sucked his nipples.

Rai's orgasm shuddered through him as he braced his hands on the edge of the tub, his cock pulsing in my fist. Feeling his body ride its release, I gave in to my own orgasm and pulled Rai in for a deep, searching kiss as I shot my load into the warm water of the bath.

When we both finally caught our breaths, Rai rested his forehead against mine. "Shower to rinse off?"

I nodded and we left the tub and climbed into the shower. Taking only enough time to wash the important bits and shampoo our hair, we rinsed quickly. Drying with big fluffy towels, we made our way to the bed and collapsed into a damp, naked heap of arms and legs, spent cocks, and slow, easy kisses.

"Sleep," I commanded and my heart warmed when Rai just smiled and nodded before drifting into dreamland.

Not meaning to sleep myself, I woke some time later with a warm and cozy Rai still sleeping in my arms. I shifted, hoping to ease the ache in my arm caught under Rai, and winced when he woke.

"Hey," he said sleepily. "How long did we sleep?"

"Not terribly long, there's still a bit of light outside." My hand trailed softly up and down his back, loving how he shivered when I teased my fingers along his ass cheeks.

"I'm probably going to be bad at it," Rai started.

I stopped him with a kiss. "You've not been bad at anything since the moment I met you."

"Okay, well, I'm willing to learn and get better," he said with a smirk as he reached between us to stroke my dick. "I want to suck you off."

I knew he felt the way my cock twitched because he smiled and bit his lip. "How about this?" I kissed him. "I suck you off first, then you can do me. I have a feeling that once I come, I'm going to crash hard, so let's have you go first."

Rai nodded and I had to laugh at how enthusiastic he seemed.

"Thoughts on swallowing? I'll warn you, but do you want me to unload in your mouth or pull out?" My cock was rock-hard and ready to get the show on the road.

"In my mouth, want to taste you," Rai licked his lips in anticipation. "What about you?"

"Wanna swallow everything you can give me," I growled. "And you can go hard if you want, I don't mind gagging a bit."

"Oh, uh, I don't know if I mind gagging," Rai answered honestly.

I kissed him. "I'll go easy, promise." I moved to the head of the bed and patted my chest. "Come here." The position was one I'd never tried; the random hookups I'd had weren't usually near a bed when a bathroom stall worked just as well.

Rai scrambled to straddle my chest, his knees pressing against the mattress by my ears and my arms coming around so I could grip his ass.

"Give it to me," I ordered. "Wanna watch you feed it between my lips."

Rai shuddered and grasped his cock before pressing it against my mouth.

I opened and took in his hard length, savoring the bitter, salty flavor of his pre-cum.

Rai whimpered and shifted to brace his hands against the headboard. "This okay?"

I nodded, my lips spread around his cock, and I pulled him hard against me so he reached the back of my throat. Rai threw his head back and moaned but began thrusting his hips, his cock sliding hard and fast between my lips.

"Not gonna last," Rai warned.

Urging him on, desperate to taste him, to feel him unload on my tongue, I gripped his ass and set a fast pace. I teased my fingers between his ass cheeks and moaned around his cock until Rai tensed and his length pulsed in my mouth, hot, salty cum coating my tongue.

Rai called my name as he gave in to his release before pulling from my mouth and collapsing next to me. "Oh, my fudging God," he panted. "I may not even care if we ever get to anal. Everything we've done has been so damn amazing."

I chuckled and gripped my dick, the memory of Rai getting off sending me close to the edge.

Rai moved between my legs and batted my hand way. "My turn," he whispered.

"Won't take long, you got me all primed and ready with that little show," I warned, grunting deep and low when Rai's sweet mouth came around my head, his tongue tentatively tasting and teasing my slit. "Oh, fuck, Rai."

What he lacked in experience, he made up for in sheer enthusiasm. His lips, tongue, and hand worked their magic. When he popped off my cock, I nearly cried.

"What's wrong?"

"I wanna be on my knees, you standing," Rai said as he moved to stand and pulled me from the bed.

Kinda loving that he knew what he wanted and wasn't afraid to ask, I let him guide me to lean against the wall before he dropped to his knees.

The image of Rai kneeling for me, his hand wrapped around my cock, deep brown eyes staring up at me as he painted my pre-cum against his lips would haunt me for the rest of my life. "Suck me," I begged.

Rai took my hard cock back between his soft, pink lips. One hand stroking with his mouth while the other hand fondled my balls and teased my taint. When he moved his hand to trail up my torso, stopping to pinch my nipples, I couldn't stop myself. I groaned and let the orgasm wash over me, loving how Rai did his best to take everything I gave him but lost a trickle of my cum from the corner of his mouth.

"My knees are gonna give out," I said, breathlessly, my cock still pulsing between his lips.

Rai let my spent dick slide from his mouth as he stood and yanked me to the bed. He reached for a towel, wiped up whatever stickiness remained from our oral session, and rolled to his back, pulling me to settle between his spread legs. "Kiss me," he demanded.

I captured his swollen lips with mine and spent the next several minutes savoring our mixed flavors and exploring his hot mouth. Eventually, knowing there was no way I was getting off again anytime soon, I rolled to his side and gathered him close. "Sleep."

"Can we play again in the morning?" Rai's words were slurred with sated exhaustion.

"Mmhm," I agreed, hating that this was just *playing* for Rai when it felt so monumental and life-changing for me.

Enjoy this time before it's gone. It will be the only thing that gets you through when you're back to being alone.

NINE
RAI

I smiled as I came awake the next morning, the sun just starting to brighten our room. I didn't want to leave and I didn't want to stop waking up in Spencer's arms. Being back in our separate beds, going back to being just friends when this whole fake-it-to-get-rid-of-Lance thing was over sucked donkey balls and it hadn't even happened.

If I let myself forget that Spencer was just doing me a favor, let myself forget that he'd never go for a guy like me, I could picture us in a real relationship. I was head-over-heels in love with my best friend—ruined for anyone else—and had no clue how to deal with the impending heartbreak.

Spencer's arms tightened around me, his erection pressed against my ass as I wriggled into him. "Good morning," he growled against my ear. "You looking for trouble?"

Chuckling, I took his hand and placed it on my hard cock. "Looking? I think I've already found it."

Spencer moaned and stroked me as he kissed my neck.

"I know you said we had to take it slow," I started, gasping when Spencer teased his thumb across my slit, "and I'm not asking for anal right now —I didn't even bring any condoms or anything—but I want you to know that I really wanna try it if you're okay with that."

He continued his stroking as he pressed his cock between my cheeks and sucked at the sensitive skin where my neck and back met. "I'm totally okay with it. Glad we don't have condoms right now because I'd for sure break my *go-slow* vow."

Heart pounding, I licked my lips. "I've never been with anyone and I know you'd tell me if there was a reason you couldn't go bare…"

"No," Spencer said gruffly. "Not even going there. This is learning and practice; I can't let you think it's okay to go bare with me when there will be others and you'll need to be smart."

My stomach hurt to think of *others*. I didn't want anyone else touching me the way Spencer did. Didn't even want to contemplate opening myself up to someone else. And the thought that Spencer may again one day share his body with another man nearly drove me to tears. "Yeah, I get it," I said thickly.

"We can do other things," Spencer promised. He shifted to grab something from the bedside table. "Keep your legs together, gonna fuck between them." He fumbled with a bottle and a light, clean fragrance filled the air.

Lotion.

Spencer slicked both hands and then moved to press his cock between my legs, his length gliding from the bottom of my crack to press against my nuts. As he thrust into me, he jerked my cock with his lotioned hand and whispered in my ear, "Keep your legs tight. Wanna watch you come and then shoot my load on your balls."

The slick friction along my crack, taint, and balls was enough to have me whimpering, but Spencer's tight fist stroking my cock nearly sent me over the edge. "Shit, shit, shit," I babbled. "Oh fudge, I'm gonna come." I rocked into his fist before pressing back onto his cock, trying to find a release in the frantic rhythm.

"Do it," Spencer bit out, "come for me, let me feel you shoot in my hand."

I tensed and threw my head back, the orgasm

rolling through me as Spencer pumped his cock between my legs. "Wanna feel you, Spence," I begged.

Releasing my cock, Spencer wrapped both arms around my body and thrust hard and fast, the head of his dick bumping my balls over and over until he growled and shot his thick, hot release on me. "Fuck, Rai," he panted in my ear as he came down from his high.

Imagining what it would be like to have Spencer's cock buried in my ass, pulsing his hot cum as he whispered my name had my spent dick attempting to make a comeback. "So good," I murmured. "Not sure I can give up this type of sex, may have to hire you on retainer," I tried to tease.

Spencer tensed behind me and I felt the moment he pulled away—literally and figuratively. "Nah, you'll find the right guy to do this with and never look back. He'll make you realize what a joke I am." He rolled from the bed. "Better get cleaned up and head out. Work tomorrow and all that." Spencer gathered his clothes and headed toward the bathroom.

When the door clicked shut, I squeezed my eyes shut and tried not to let the tears flow. He clearly didn't want me with him. Very clearly didn't want to think about having sex with me outside of our little fake boyfriend deal. God, I wanted *more* with Spencer so badly I could taste it, could imagine our future together. But I had to accept it wasn't meant to be.

Spencer didn't see me like that. And, even if he did, he didn't see himself in any type of positive light. I'd never force him to be with me if he truly didn't want to, but a small part of me kept hope alive that *maybe* he could learn to love me while learning to love himself as well.

He finished his shower and told me to take my time because he'd warm up last night's dinner for our breakfast.

When I emerged from the shower, he gestured toward the food. "Leftover pizza, noodles, and burritos, plus the cupcakes we never got to. Breakfast of champions."

I smiled—determined to forget about the whole fake situation—and wrapped my arms around his neck, kissing him slow and easy. "Thanks. You're so good to me." *I love you so damn much* I wanted to say. But I'd already pushed him away with talk of continuing our little setup, I didn't want to push him further with words I was positive he felt he didn't deserve and very likely couldn't return.

Spencer smiled against my lips and deepened the

kiss for a split second before pulling away, a flash of *something* crossing his face. "Better eat up so we can hit the road."

I swallowed thickly. "Yeah, back to reality."

"HOW WAS YOUR VISIT WITH ALICIA?" I asked Spencer as we settled into our very lonely, very separate beds a couple weeks later. As much as I *wanted* to be in his bed, I hadn't been able to figure out an actual reason to be there other than just being selfish. So, I made do with sleeping alone and longing for Spencer's arms around me.

"It was good. I like her. The cookies and tea are always a nice touch," Spencer answered.

I'd called and set up a joint meet-and-greet type appointment with the therapist and since then, we'd both seen her twice.

"She has all these ideas about how I should embrace my imperfections and make a choice to love myself." He snorted as if to dismiss the suggestion, but his voice held a wistful tone. "Gave me some quote about choices or some shit like that."

Wishing I could hold him as he processed through Alicia's advice, I snuggled under my blanket. "What was the quote?"

"Said I can choose to love myself—see the good in myself and allow myself to choose happiness." Spencer huffed. "I guess some guy named John C. Maxwell said, 'Life is a matter of choices, and every choice you make makes you,'" he said. "Like a person can just *choose* to be happy. *Choose* to ignore all the shit that's wrong with them."

We were silent for a while.

"You know, there's a Japanese philosophy that fits perfectly with what Alicia is trying to get you to understand," I started, not wanting to push, but needing the bits and pieces of healing I'd started seeing in Spencer to grow into more; Alicia had already been good for him. I wanted so badly to see him love himself—even if that meant we stayed nothing but friends, it would be completely worth it.

"Yeah?" Spencer grunted.

"Mmhm, it's called *wabi-sabi*."

"Wabi-sabi?" I heard the grin in Spencer's words. "Sounds funny, what's it mean?"

"Well, put in the simplest of terms, it gives you the permission to be yourself. Encourages you to embrace the perfection of being imperfectly you."

Spencer was quiet for a long time. "Wish it was that easy. Don't know that I could ever do it." He rolled to his side, facing me in the darkness of our room. "Tell me more about it."

"Well, like I said, it's a Japanese philosophy that encourages us to focus on the blessings hiding in our daily lives and to celebrate the way things *are* rather than how we think they *should* be." I reached for my phone and searched for more about wabi-sabi and began to read. "'Wabi is said to be defined as "rustic simplicity" or "understated elegance" with a focus on a less-is-more mentality. Sabi is translated to "taking pleasure in the imperfect." Wabi-sabi understands the tender, raw beauty of a gray December landscape and the aching elegance of an abandoned building or shed. It celebrates cracks and crevices and rot and all the other marks that time and weather and use leave behind. To discover wabi-sabi is to see the singular beauty in something that may first look decrepit and ugly.'"

"Don't know why I can appreciate the imperfections of others, accept the imperfections of an old house just needing some love and repair, but it's so much harder to let go of my own failures and mistakes," Spencer said gruffly.

"For some reason, I think it's easier to let others off the hook than it is to do the same for ourselves."

Just when I thought Spencer had shut down—ready to avoid the tough conversations as usual—or gone to sleep, he cleared his throat. "Hadley was super cute asking you to read your Japanese storybooks to her tonight."

I smiled into the darkness as I recalled the evening of dinner and reading and laughter with our friends and family. "She was. I'll have to keep those around. Too bad she fell asleep on that last one, it's one of my favorites from when I was little."

"Would you read it to me?" Spencer asked, his voice filled with longing and trepidation, as if he was preparing for me to judge him or reject him.

My heart hurt to think of Spencer as a little kid with no one taking care of him, no one reading to him and keeping him safe, no one making him feel loved and protected.

"Sure," I answered. I clicked on the tiny reading lamp next to my bed and rummaged in the pile of books I'd brought from home. "Where did I stop?"

"The dad didn't believe the daughter about the tiny warriors coming to her room at night so he stayed awake to watch for them," Spencer answered sleepily.

I began to read from *The Toothpick Warriors*. I read about how the father noticed all the toothpicks in his daughter's room and realized that tiny warriors had been coming to her room at night to use the toothpicks as swords. The daughter admitted to her very bad habit with the toothpicks and promised to never be so lazy again. "'She never forgot the tiny warriors, and if she ever used a toothpick again, you may be sure she was very careful to throw it away properly.'" I closed the book and glanced over to Spencer before turning off the light.

I was sure he'd fallen asleep, so I jumped when he spoke. "Maybe her bad habit, the thing keeping her awake and making her sick, is kinda like me not being able to accept my imperfections. The father is like you and Alicia, telling me how I can fix it and make things better." He stopped talking and a soft snore filled the room.

Fighting the urge to crawl into his bed and pull him close, kiss away his doubts and fears, I smiled and snuggled deep under my blanket. Maybe Spencer would eventually find his way to loving himself after all.

"WOW, THIS IS PRETTY NICE," Spencer said as we took in our room at the gaming tournament in Indianapolis.

My body thrummed. There was once again only the one bed—anticipation and guilt warred in my head because I *may* have purposely made the reservation that way this time around. "Yeah, I wasn't sure what to expect, but it's a really nice room."

We only had Saturday and Sunday at the event, so just the one night—which was actually good because the room was pricey—but I seriously wanted to lock the door and keep Spencer in bed the whole time. To hell with the tournament.

We'd had a few touches here and there since the ski trip, and a hot make out session in one of the game shop's back rooms when Lance had been around—honestly though, I'd lost myself to the kiss so completely, I hadn't even realized when Lance had left—but *fake* boyfriends had no reason to touch, kiss, cuddle, and have sex when there was no show to put on. So, knowing that I had two days with Spencer had me nearly bursting with anticipation.

"We've got an hour until the first game," I said as I wrapped my arms around his neck. "Care to impart some wisdom and give me some time to practice?"

Spencer's jaw bulged and for a moment, I expected him to say no, but he closed his eyes and pulled me close. "Nothing new, but practicing already-learned skills can be arranged." His mouth came down on mine and I gasped at the ferocity and heat between us.

God, how I'd missed his touch, missed his flavor, his lips on mine. I walked backward to the bed.

"Naked, need you naked," I murmured against his lips.

We stripped in a flurry and fell onto the bed, laughing and kissing. How could something we both knew was fake seem so right and so real?

"Maybe I lied about nothing new," Spencer growled as he tongued my nipple. "You up for some extra credit?"

I whimpered as his teeth grazed my collarbone. "If it involves your cock in my mouth, I'm all for it."

Spencer maneuvered our bodies so our mouths were level with each other's cock. "This okay?" He fisted my cock and swirled his tongue around my head.

"Fudge, yeah," I groaned before licking a wet strip along his shaft and taking him between my lips.

We fell into a perfect rhythm of rocking hips and sucking mouths. Spencer paused long enough to slick his finger with spit before pressing his digit against my hole as he continued to swallow my cock.

I'd played with my ass before and knew the stretch and sting could take away my breath in one moment and send me spiraling into bliss the next. Spencer's finger breaching my tight ring was no different. I gasped at the quick burn, but quickly savored the fullness as my balls drew up tight and my cock begged for release.

I tightened my grip on Spencer's cock—I'd learned he liked a heavy touch—and sucked him deep to the back of my throat. He moaned around my length and pressed a second finger into my heat just as my release overtook me. I thrust my cock hard and deep into Spencer's mouth, knowing he'd take everything I could give him, and hummed around his throbbing shaft. Within seconds, Spencer tensed and shot his load onto my tongue as he groaned my name.

When we both could breathe, he rearranged our bodies and pulled me against his chest. "A plus," he whispered into my hair.

"Well, we didn't make the best use of our time," I teased. "We still have forty-five minutes until the game starts."

"I should be embarrassed about that, but it was so hot I can't even bring myself to feel bad." He sighed as he stroked a hand up and down my back.

"Never embarrassed, that was way too good."

"Set your alarm, we'll sleep a bit," Spencer said.

With thirty minutes to doze, I settled into Spencer's arms as if I'd found my home.

I want this. Want this man, want this to be real.

My sinuses stung as the thought washed over me.

What if I just told Spencer the truth? Told him that —while I really did want to get rid of Lance—part of me had been selfish in suggesting the fake boyfriend thing because I'd hoped it would bring us together and give me a part of Spencer I knew I'd never get otherwise. Would he be okay with that? Feel tricked? Feel used?

I cuddled deeper into Spencer's warm chest as I recalled Cooper's words. *"Spencer doesn't really know how to do the whole relationship thing. I don't think it's so much about him not liking* you *as it is about him not knowing how to like and accept himself."*

Spencer was making strides in his work with Alicia, even in such a short time. Would he be ready for something *real* with me yet?

I sighed. I wished there was an easy answer. Wished Spencer could just choose to believe in himself and let me love him.

How do you know he can't or won't?

Honestly?

I knew the answer and had a pretty good idea where it came from.

Fear.

Fear controlled me. If I kept quiet, I could have this—even fake—for a bit longer. If I told Spencer how I felt, I risked losing him even sooner.

The last time I'd owned up to something, told the truth for the sake of being my real self, I'd lost my family.

I wasn't sure I could survive losing Spencer if my truth was too much for him.

When my alarm went off a bit later, I moaned sleepily because I hadn't been able to doze at all.

"Let's get going. You've got games to win." Spencer bounded from the bed and went to the bathroom to wash off before getting dressed.

Once we headed to the elevator, my melancholy had somewhat dissipated. "You don't have to stay and watch me the whole time."

"Nah, figured that would be annoying. Thought I'd let Lance see us and get you settled, then I'll go take a look at the other things in the convention hall. Sounds like there's quite a few events going on; maybe some are free or the gaming bracelet will get me in the door."

Twenty minutes later, we'd put on our little show for a sneering Lance—although, it would have been a lie to say I didn't savor every moment of those kisses —and Spencer had wished me luck before he left me to play my game.

I settled in and had a lot of fun playing, but I couldn't help thinking about what Spencer was doing and wishing we could just ditch the tournament and hang out. One thing I noticed was that Lance was less obnoxious with his come-ons and spent a lot more of his time flirting with one of the newer guys in the gaming group.

For a moment, I watched to see if the new guy seemed put off by Lance, but the more I observed, the more I realized the new guy appeared to be the one going after Lance.

Hmmm, interesting development. But whatever, I'd take it if it meant Lance would leave me alone.

Fudge.

If Lance was into someone else and moved on from his obsession with me, that would mean Spencer and I had no reason to continue the fake boyfriend set-up.

I swallowed hard and tried to keep from feeling like the bottom had just fallen out of my world. Was it wrong to keep the news from Spencer for just a bit longer? We still had the cohort dinner to attend. Could I keep the ruse going until then? Every moment with Spencer was a memory in the making and I needed to stockpile them.

A few hours later, Spencer came back to the gaming area while I was packing up. "Hey, how'd you do?"

I smiled at his genuine interest—he wasn't much into the game I'd been playing, but I loved that he wanted to support me. Fake boyfriend or not, he was a good friend. "I won a few, but not enough to make it to the final round tomorrow." I honestly wasn't even upset; the game didn't mean a fraction to me what Spencer did, and I was grateful to have the rest of the weekend with him.

His face fell, but he schooled it quickly. "Oh, so are you wanting to leave?"

"What? No way." I hooked my arm in his as we headed from the room. "We've got the room and we both planned to be gone the whole weekend. I say we make the most of it." I was desperate to cement his scent, his touch, his smile in my head and heart. Sure, I'd still have his smile when we were back to just friends, but it hurt to think of everything else I'd be giving up.

"I'm down. I'm sorry you didn't make it further in your game."

I waved him off. "Nah, it wasn't that big of a deal. I signed up for it back when I was so excited to have some money and time to spend. The actual game and winning didn't mean that much to me, but having the chance to just breathe and enjoy myself is a big plus." In truth, I'd been distracted during the game. Wondering about Spencer, watching to see if Lance was watching me or his new guy, begging the universe to let me have a little more time with Spencer. It wasn't a surprise that I didn't advance past the first round. "Did you find anything interesting while you waited?"

"Actually, I did. You wanna get something to eat? Then I'll show you. There's this big craft and hobby show you might like. Plus, a few other things." Spencer steered me toward a little food court area. "What's your pick?"

I studied the choices, my lips pursed as I tried to decide. "It's so hard," I whined.

Spencer groaned. "Don't talk about things being hard or I'll yank you up the elevator and keep you in bed until checkout tomorrow."

Eyes wide and blood rushing south, I blinked several times. "First, I was talking about the *difficulty* of making a decision. Second, let's go. Eating is overrated; I need all the lessons I can get before I lose my tutor."

I wanted to believe there was real disappointment in Spencer's eyes, but it disappeared so quickly that I had to think it was just my hopeful imagination.

"Nah, let's eat and look around. We've got all night and the morning. It's not like there's much else for me to teach you. You've learned the basics; now you just find the right guy and spend the rest of your life perfecting." Spencer pointed to a table and dropped his bag in the chair. "I'll save our seats if you want to grab the food?"

We decided to split two meals—I picked a sub sandwich with chips and Spencer opted for a box of chicken nuggets and fries—and I went to get in line. While I waited, my phone buzzed. *Ten dollars from Spencer Nelson.* I smiled and looked toward him, only to have my heart melt at the smirk and nod he sent my way. There was *no way* Spencer didn't feel at least a little bit of what I felt for him.

Did he and Cooper have their own little secret joke of trading ten dollars back and forth? Did Spencer take off of work to spend weekends with Cooper? Did he spend hours at night talking to Cooper and asking him to read stories to him?

I wasn't jealous of Cooper at all. I adored the guy and I was glad Spencer had Cooper in his life. But my head and heart were at war; surely the way Spencer acted with me—which was so different than how he acted with Cooper, or even Jesse or Dalton— was a tiny indication that maybe he felt something for me.

Right?

"You've learned the basics; now you just find the right guy and spend the rest of your life perfecting."

Spencer's words crashed into me as I fumbled through my order of a turkey, ham, and bacon sub with cheese, cucumbers, avocado, and spicy mustard.

I didn't *want* to find the *right* guy. I'd found the

damn right guy. He just didn't realize it or feel the same.

I wasn't a fudging prude, it wasn't like I'd been holding onto my virginity for marriage or anything like that. But now that I'd shared such intimate moments with Spencer, I had absolutely zero desire to open myself up to anyone else in that way. Maybe in the future? When the hurt had lessened?

Maybe.

But I didn't want to contemplate a future without Spencer. And not just having him as a friend; I wanted the real deal. Wanted to spend the rest of my life learning and loving with Spencer. Not learning from him and then being pawned off on someone else for the loving part.

I ordered the box of twenty nuggets and fries plus two large cokes as I continued to ruminate on the decisions before me.

Play out the fake boyfriend thing. Call it quits. Go back to being friends.

Be miserable.

Or…

Tell the truth. Let Spencer know exactly how I felt. Turn what we had into something real.

Live happily ever after.

I huffed as I waited for my order.

There were about a hundred variations of those

two options and I hated not knowing how any of them would actually play out.

If I *knew* how Spencer felt, the decisions would be easier. Maybe not easier to accept—if he didn't feel the same—but at least easier to make.

Thanking the weary-looking employee for the food, I headed back to sit with Spencer. We dug into our food, splitting the sandwich, chips, nuggets, and fries like an old married couple without a single thought. Chatting and laughing as we ate, I couldn't help but let myself live the fantasy, believe that it was real—at least *some* of it had to be, right?

"You ever hear of Residential Renovation and Repair?" Spencer asked as he dunked a nugget in a cup of sauce.

Brow furrowed, I gave it some thought. "I don't *think* so? Why?"

He shrugged. "They've got a booth set up in one of the smaller venues. It's like a home improvement event I guess. Anyway, the Residential booth caught my eye and I wandered over. Not one hundred percent sure what they do, but I know they're located all over the country. Kinda like a union, but not? I gathered they're kinda like a management company maybe?" He ran a hand through his hair. "Honestly, I didn't want to ask tons of questions for fear of getting roped into something." Spencer took a drink. "Seems like they provide leads for jobs, help contractors get insurance, assist with workers comp claims, and give loans for equipment, that type of thing—and I'm sure take a pretty penny in their cut."

I nodded along as he spoke, not completely following where he was going with the story.

"The guy working the booth said he knew my name," Spencer offered, almost shyly.

"Like, knew you from school or something?"

He shook his head and chomped a few fries. "No, he was asking me what I did—I guess some of my questions and answers clued him in that I worked in or near construction of some sort—and I told him I worked on houses."

Spencer hadn't yet been able to give up on sounding disgusted with his career most of the time, but he had at least started *sometimes* not looking embarrassed or ashamed of what he did. Baby steps.

"So, he asked if I was an independent contractor or if I worked for a company. I told him the company and he asked where I was based. Told him that and he asked if my name was Spencer Nelson by any chance."

My eyes went wide. "Impressive. Or creepy?"

Spencer chuckled. "I would have chalked it up to the damn name tags they have us wearing, but it only shows first name. I probably got a little suspicious and stuttered for a bit, but I finally got around to asking how he knew my name." His flushed cheeks told me he was both shocked and pleased, even if he was trying to downplay it. "Said they keep up with the big names and try to track the employees who are either the most successful for a company or seem to be a good bet to go independent. I'm sure they do it just so they can get their claws into them and make money, but it felt kinda good to know my name was on their radar—for something good, no less. Never really had that kind of thing happen." He shrugged. "I know it's not much, but..."

"Stop." I reached over and caressed his hand. "I don't want to hear a *this really cool thing happened to me but I'm going to downplay it* type story. Your skills and hard work are being recognized and that's amazing. Maybe you're not interested in what this company has to offer, but you should feel really proud right now." I gave his hand a squeeze before returning to my food. "And for what it's worth, I'm proud of you."

Shiny brown eyes caught mine and held. "Knowing you're proud of me is always worth something, don't ever doubt that."

We ate in silence for a few moments.

"Do you think you'd ever want to go independent? Have your own business?" I asked.

Spencer shrugged. "Yes and no. There's a lot of appeal to having my own business. Picking my own hours, choosing the projects I want to work on, hiring the best people for my team. But then again, there's the downside of not having a big company name behind me, providing insurance, hiring and firing. Going independent means I'd kinda have to be a one-man-show."

"Unless you work with a company like that Residential one you spoke to?"

"Yeah," Spencer nodded, "but working with a company like that means them taking a cut. Building a name for myself would take a while and giving them a cut doesn't sit well when I'd already be making less—at least in the beginning."

"Could you continue with your company but take on independent jobs on the side as you build your name and reputation?" I really had no clue how any of his job worked, but I loved hearing him talk about his work.

Spencer gathered his trash. "Yeah, some of the guys do that. I work a lot of overtime; I could cut back to just regular time and use my spare hours to do independent work."

"Might be worth checking out the need in

Remington and surrounding areas. May be some people who aren't interested or can't afford a company name, but they'd gladly pay an individual for quality work. And you'd get to pick and choose which projects you worked on." I wadded up my sub wrapper and chip bag before standing.

"Yeah, it's not a bad idea," Spencer mused.

We tossed our trash and headed to check out the craft show.

Within an hour, I was done with booths and crafts and just wanted to go to the room.

"Can we call it quits?" I asked.

Spencer nodded and we headed toward the elevators.

Once back in the room, I dropped my bag and stripped off my shirt. "I want to shower, nap, and have sex."

Spencer's eyes went wide, but he smiled. "I like a man who knows what he wants."

"Give me about twenty minutes and then join me," I answered as I removed the rest of my clothes and went to turn on the shower. I'd practice with the prep once at home just to be ready for the real deal.

After taking care of necessary preparations, I hollered for Spencer to come in. Unable to take my eyes off his gorgeous naked body, I licked my lips and

stepped aside so he could join me under the warm
water.

"Wanna suck you off," I whispered against his
lips as I wrapped my arms around his neck.

"Well, that works perfectly," Spencer teased as he
nibbled at my bottom lip, "because I wanna suck you
off, so we can take turns." He pushed me against the
tile and plunged his tongue into my mouth as he
stroked my cock.

We kissed for several moments before I broke
away, panting. "Please," I begged.

Spencer gave a seductive smile and trailed
kisses from my jaw down my chest and abs until
he settled on his knees and buried his nose in my
groin. Nipping, nuzzling, and pressing kisses
against my hot, wet skin, Spencer teased me
while cupping my balls. "Love sucking you, love
tasting this perfect cock," he murmured before
swirling his tongue around my head, making me
gasp.

"Please, Spence, wanna feel you. Wanna come." I
rocked my hips, encouraging him to stroke me, suck
me, *something*.

Gazing up at me, his eyes locked on mine,
Spencer guided my cock to his lips and sucked me
deep. Dropping my head back against the shower
wall, I groaned and reached down to grip his hair.

"Yeah, pull my hair, fuck my face," Spencer demanded before taking me between his lips again.

Super rough sex wasn't one of my kinks—at least not from what I'd learned so far—but I did enjoy watching Spencer's cheeks hollow out and his eyes water as I thrust my cock hard and fast into his hot mouth. Tightening my hold on his hair, loving the way he hummed around my shaft, I increased my pace as Spencer toyed with my balls and teased a finger into my crack. With his hot, wet mouth on my dick, his finger dipping in and out of my ass, and the promise that I'd soon be on my knees sucking him deep, I tensed and shot my release onto his tongue.

Spencer savored what I gave him until my cock stopped pulsing. Then he let my spent dick slip from his mouth before standing and capturing my lips, plunging his tongue deep.

"My turn," I whispered, biting his bottom lip and licking to soothe the sting.

Spencer gave me another long, soul-searing kiss before I spun him to press his chest against the tile wall and dropped to my knees. Spreading his gorgeous ass cheeks, I leaned in and placed tiny kisses against his pucker, smiling when Spencer groaned and bucked his hips.

"Fuck, Rai," he growled.

Encouraged by his response, I tongued his hole,

pressing into his tight ring as I reached around to stroke his cock. "You wanna come like this or in my mouth," I asked over the gentle rush of the shower.

"Too much to decide, do what feels best for you, gonna blow either way," Spencer panted, thrusting his cock into my fist and his ass onto my tongue.

As much as I loved the thought of him getting off on the rimming, I craved his cock between my lips and his taste on my tongue. I grabbed his hips and spun him around, trailing my tongue up his thick shaft, teasing the protruding vein. With a flick of my tongue against his slit, I took him in my mouth. Shifting to keep his cock sliding between my lips while still being able to stare up into Spencer's eyes, I bobbed my head on his shaft, loving the look of ecstasy on his face.

"Fuck, Rai. Fuck, that's good. Love your mouth, fuck, I'm gonna come so hard," he babbled.

Gripping Spencer's ass, I teased my fingers between his cheeks and pressed against his hole while he rocked his hips, an obscene groan escaping him. Working the tip of my finger into his pucker, I hummed around his cock when he tensed and increased his speed.

With one hand twisting his balls and one hand stroking my hair, Spencer threw his head back and moaned my name as the first spurts of cum coated my tongue. When he pulled from my mouth, Spencer winced. "Damn you worked me over good. Good thing you want to sleep, not sure I'm functional right now."

Turning off the water, I climbed from the shower and grabbed two big, fluffy towels. "We'll sleep. Gotta rest and recharge for the main event. *That* was just a warm-up," I teased.

"Fuck, what is this? Some sort of *the student has become the teacher* type thing?" Spencer pulled me close, wrapping us both in the softness of his towel as he kissed my neck. He nuzzled my jawline and moved ever-so-slowly to capture my lips, dipping his tongue into my mouth and growling when I slid my tongue—likely still tasting of his release—against his. "That was amazing, so damn good," he murmured against my lips.

"Everything we do is good," I quipped. *We should keep doing it and not let it end.*

"Well, let's take a good nap and get ready for the real deal." Spencer started to push me from the bathroom, but he paused, his arms wrapped around me, chest pressed to my back, catching my eyes in the mirror. "Hey, you know that what we've been doing is sex, right? We don't *have* to have anal to count it as *real* sex, nothing has to go any further."

I took hold of his arm and nodded, my eyes never

leaving his. "I know. And I've loved everything we've done. But I *want* to experience it, wanna feel you inside me."

Spencer's eyes darkened and he gave a quick nod. "Okay, as long as you're not feeling obligated."

"Never." *I want everything with you, need to feel you stretching me open, have you leave your mark on me. Never want to let you go.*

We made our way to the bed and tumbled onto the mattress, Spencer spooning behind me and pulling the comforter up to our shoulders.

TEN
SPENCER

I WOKE WITH A START, the remnants of a dream that Rai left me leaving me unsettled. But he was right there, cuddled into me, breathing softly. Asleep like I should have been. Based on the clock on the bedside table, I'd only slept for about an hour.

We probably needed to get some food and I figured Rai wouldn't want to sleep too long since it would mess with his overnight sleep.

But I was loath to wake him.

If I let him sleep, I could pretend the whole charade didn't exist. Could keep pretending it was real. Rai's smile, his hand in mine, his warm body wrapped in my arms, the little whimpers he made when he shot his load on my tongue...I wanted all of those things and more to be *mine*. Not mine for as long as it took to convince Lance to move along. *Mine* for real and forever.

Thanks to the few sessions I'd had with Alicia—and it probably helped that Bev, Cooper, Rai, and others had been pounding the same shit into my head since I'd known them—I was taking very tiny baby steps toward...well, I wasn't exactly sure what I was moving toward. *Accepting myself* or *loving myself* seemed a bit too farfetched, at least for now. My past still haunted me and I couldn't ever see a time when I'd feel worthy of love, from myself or others. *But* Alicia's words and the exercises she had me do—no matter how stupid they made me feel—stuck with me. Maybe I was moving toward making the choice to at least allow others to love me. It didn't make sense that anyone could look at me and see someone worthy of more than a passing glance, but there were no doubt people in my life who wanted to love me.

I liked what Rai had told me about wabi-sabi. Celebrating my imperfections would be a mix of difficult and easy. Easy to recognize the imperfections, difficult to celebrate them. But the fact that there was a whole philosophy built on welcoming and accepting imperfections was kinda calming for me.

Would I ever be able to wrap my head around a guy like Rai maybe liking me for real? It seemed impossible, felt as if there was no way I deserved it. But I wanted two things more than I wanted my next breath.

One, I wanted Rai to see me as someone he could love, someone he could spend the rest of his life with.

Two—a choice I was trying my best to make—I wanted to be able to accept Rai loving me.

I sighed and kissed the top of his head.

Maybe I was being ridiculous thinking there was any chance he could ever love me. But try as I might to convince myself this whole thing between us was a ruse and just two guys taking advantage of a situation to get our rocks off, there was this little sliver of my head and heart that kept insisting it was more. What Rai and I had was more than a fake relationship, more than just me teaching him about sex.

I felt it in my soul.

But I didn't know how to broach the subject with Rai.

If my past had taught me anything, it was that good things don't last and people don't stay around.

What did Alicia tell you? You need to focus on the good things that have *lasted and the people who* have *stayed.* Choose *to see the good and move on from the bad.*

What if I brought it up to Rai? Told him how I

was feeling and asked if he wanted to ditch the fake thing and try this for real—honestly, would anything even change? The only thing that seemed fake about the whole situation was our insistence that it was just temporary and just for show.

But what if he laughed? What if the worst of my imagination came to fruition and Rai sneered at me? Told me he was just in it for the sex and to get Lance off his back, none of what we'd done had meant anything to him?

I wasn't at a place, mentally or emotionally, to survive that just yet.

In your heart of hearts, do you really think Rai would do that?

I wanted to think he wouldn't, but deep-seated fears and self-loathing were hard things to break through.

Maybe it was for the best to let him go. Work on myself a bit more. Hope that he was still available when I was feeling a little stronger and less vulnerable.

You really think a guy like Rai isn't going to be snatched up faster than you can blink?

I closed my eyes and breathed out slowly.

Tell Rai and risk losing him even sooner than planned?

Keep my feelings to myself and lose him anyway?

I was a damn construction worker, what could I possibly offer to a guy like Rai?

That guy today seemed impressed by your work. Rai is always proud of your work. Maybe give him a bit more credit and let him decide if what you can offer is enough for him?

God, it was a lot easier when my head and heart were just as disgusted with me as I was. Now that they were getting on board with Alicia's exercises and advice, it was harder and harder to cling to the *I'm not good enough for him* argument.

Maybe clinging to that was the only thing I had the mental and emotional energy for.

Maybe clinging to that is why you're mentally and emotionally exhausted.

I pushed the thought away, once again playing ostrich, but another thought waltzed into my head.

Lance.

I'd seen him earlier in the day, being all flirty with a guy in the game group—a guy who seemed all too into the attention.

If Lance moved on, Rai and I were done. Goal met.

Had Rai noticed Lance and this new guy? Jerry, I think I saw on his name tag.

Should I ask?

No, the ostrich routine was working fine and

bringing it up now would possibly ruin the cohort dinner scheduled for the next week.

I'd enjoy what Rai and I had for the remaining time.

Then I'd let him go like originally planned.

As much as I selfishly wanted to believe he and I could be more, it wasn't fair of me to change up the agenda. Rai had presented the whole scheme to me as a way to get Lance to back off—which looked to be happening—and a fun, easy way for him to experience sex with someone he trusted. Check.

Rai could move on and find happiness with someone better than me.

We could go back to being friends.

You're an idiot if you think that's ever going to happen.

It was the right thing to do by Rai.

Maybe let him decide what's right for him?

Letting him decide meant opening myself up and I wasn't ready for another person I loved to let me down.

You're going to be heartbroken either way, why not take the risk and tell him how you feel? At least that way you'll know you tried.

With heavy eyes and a heavier heart, I pulled Rai closer and drifted back to sleep. The ostrich routine was one thing I was getting really good at.

RAI ROLLED in my arms to face me. He planted kisses on my collarbone and teased my nipples as I blinked awake. "Hey," he whispered, smiling up at me.

Instantly turned on and wanting more—would I *ever* not want more with this man?—I caressed my hand up and down his back. "Sleep okay?"

"I'll be pissed tonight when I can't fall asleep, but the nap was amazing." Rai brought his hand to my back and trailed short nails down my spine.

A shiver traveled through me and I tipped his mouth up to meet mine. "Maybe we need to wear you out?" Brushing a soft kiss over his pretty pink lips, I palmed his ass and pulled him close, our hard cocks pressing together.

"Mmm," Rai hummed into my mouth, his tongue delving deep. "That sounds promising."

Pressing Rai to his back, loving in the way his legs opened so I could settle between them, I rocked my hips. We both groaned as our cocks rubbed together and I reached between us. Taking us both in hand, I stroked our leaking shafts. "You know we can get off just like this and we'd both be happy and satisfied." I never wanted Rai to feel like he *had* to have anal sex to meet some sort of checklist.

"We could and we would." Rai thrust his cock into my fist and moaned when I thumbed his slit. "And if you're not into it, we don't have to go further. But I want to try it and you're the only person I'd trust to try it with."

I rolled from the bed and grabbed lube and a condom before rushing back and settling between his legs again. How was it that our bodies seemed to fit so damn perfectly? "You wanna be on top for the first time? Might give you a little more control over everything."

Rai shook his head. "Maybe tomorrow or next time?"

Please, let there be a next time.

"On your knees or like this?" I rocked my hips, praying he wanted the more impersonal doggy-style, but wanting so badly to take him on his back. Legs spread, face-to-face, intimate in a way I'd never shared with another person.

"Like this." He writhed under me. "Please."

Suddenly nervous, knowing I wasn't the most experienced and I'd definitely never had the responsibility of making someone's first time feel good, I pressed my forehead to his.

"You okay? Seriously, you don't have to. I know I'm far from your type," Rai muttered.

"Stop saying that. You're perfect and this is fine."

I planted a kiss on his lips. "Just got hit with nerves that I don't really know what I'm doing aside from a hard and fast fuck in a bathroom stall. Don't want to hurt you, wanna make it good."

"Everything we've done has been good," Rai reassured. "I know it might be a little uncomfortable, but I've taken your fingers—I've used my own fingers—I know you'll stretch me the best you can." He cupped my face. "I trust you and I want this."

Nodding, I pushed aside everything—worry that I'd hurt him, worry that it wouldn't be good for him, worry that my heart was going to shatter when I lost him—and focused only on Rai. I grabbed a pillow and shoved it under his hips.

With Rai's legs spread wide, his gorgeous ass open for me, I moved to press kisses on his cheeks before sliding my tongue from his taint to the top of his crack and back. Teasing his balls with my tongue, I smiled when Rai groaned.

"Fudge, Spence, please," he begged.

"Please what? Whatdya want?" I teased.

"Your tongue, fingers, *something*."

"Impatient." I swirled my tongue around his rim, giving him what he wanted.

"That, yeah, that," he babbled.

I continued to tongue-fuck his ass, loving the way

he writhed and moaned at my touch. "You want my fingers?"

"I want your cock," he panted.

"Fingers first." I pressed one finger against his soft, wet hole and worked it in slowly. The clench of his muscle around me made me shudder as I thought of how tight he'd be on my cock.

"God, that's good. Give me more," Rai begged.

Adding another finger, I reached up to stroke his cock, trailing my fingers through the slick precum gathering on his belly. My tongue and fingers worked his hole, my digits sliding deep and brushing over his prostate.

"Oh shit, shit, shit. Please want your cock. Need you in me."

"Can you take a third?" I asked.

Rai whimpered and bucked his hips. "Yeah, give it to me and then get your damn cock inside me."

The addition of a third finger brought a keening moan from Rai and I stretched him only long enough to ensure he could take my cock without too much discomfort. Grabbing the condom, I ripped it open and rolled it on, gripping hard to get myself under control. Slicking myself and Rai's hole with lube, I lined up my cock with his entrance and began a slow press into him.

Rai panted and moaned with each inch I gave

him. His erection flagged and I worried the pain was too much.

"You okay?" I asked through gritted teeth.

"Mmhm. Burns, but feels so good. So full."

"You're doing good, stretching for me, taking my cock so deep," I praised as his body adjusted to the invasion and allowed me to sink in bit-by-bit. "So fucking hot and tight."

"Love your cock, but glad it's not bigger," Rai panted. "Oh fuuuudge," he moaned when my balls pressed against his ass, his cock coming back to life between us.

"Good?" I shifted forward, bringing us face-to-face, cupping his cheek and brushing a kiss against his lips.

"So good," Rai whispered, his tongue teasing mine and his teeth nibbling at my bottom lip. "You can go harder."

"Don't really want this to be hard and fast—ends up over way too quick." I snaked my arms under his and held his head in my hands. "Wrap your legs around me."

Rai obeyed and pulled me even deeper when his ankles locked around my waist. "Oh damn, that's so good."

Leveraging myself on my elbows, I thrust long and slow into Rai's body, savoring every breathy whimper, obscene moan, and keening cry escaping him. "You think you can come like this?"

"Hell yeah, so damn close already. Never had my prostate hit so much, gonna blow soon."

"Good, me too." I increased my thrusts, pulling almost all the way out before sliding back in as deep as I could go. The tight heat of Rai's ass was almost more than I could handle. His noises, his hands on my back and ass, his pre-cum-slick dick pressed between us had me nearly over the edge. "Wanna feel you come on me, feel your ass tight around my cock while I shoot in you."

Rai whimpered and tightened his legs around me. With a hand on the back of my head, he pulled me in for a sloppy, sexy kiss as his cock pulsed hot spurts between us.

With his ass clenching around my throbbing cock, I thrust hard and fast three more times before burying myself and groaning as an orgasm washed over me. After several moments, my balls drained and breathing attempting to return to normal, I sighed and pressed my forehead against Rai's.

We stayed still and quiet, savoring the high for nearly a minute.

"I don't want to lose this," I whispered, my spent cock still buried in his heat.

Something passed over Rai's face. Longing? Fear?

I couldn't tell, but it was quickly replaced with a soft smile. "Same, feels too good. Maybe if I'm not too sore, we can go again in the morning?"

Tell him. Tell him that's not what you meant.

But I cleared my throat. "Yeah, probably better make the most of our time. Not sure the housemates would appreciate our lessons continuing at home." The moment broken, I let the ostrich façade take over.

Rai scoffed, his words tight. "Not like we don't hear Dalton and Gabby going at it. They really think the music covers it up?"

I chuckled. "Well, best to make the most of our time anyway. Won't have our little fuck-buddies situation for much longer." Like sixty-grit sandpaper over the coarsest of wood, my words were rough on my tongue. Hating myself for my cowardice, I pretended not to see the hurt look on Rai's face as I slipped from his body and gathered him in my arms. "Wanna shower and eat? Maybe watch a movie until we're sleepy again?"

Rai nodded against my chest where my heart used to be.

We went through the motions of showering and eating—I wasn't sure if Rai was feeling as down as me, but I hated that we both seemed off after what should have been something special. And it *was* special, at least to me, but not being able to outwardly indicate it had been monumental was really difficult.

We settled into bed—Rai seemed clingy and it worked perfectly because I didn't want to let him go —and pretended to watch a movie. Before too long, we ended up talking about the exercises Alicia had us doing.

Rai and I had different issues, but we found we'd been doing some of the same things in therapy.

"So, I liked the one where she had me ditch toxic family. Wrote down my mom and dad, my grandparents, extended family—all the people who made me feel less than worthy of their love, not good enough, a failure, like something was wrong with me—and I got to rip them up and burn them." Rai chuckled. "Alicia took me out back for the burning part. Said she didn't have a problem with burning rather than just throwing away, but she worried about the smoke detectors."

I smiled and pressed a kiss against his head. "Yeah, that one was good. My main one was my mom, but it felt good to kinda have permission to let go." I shifted and pulled the blanket up some more. "She's had me working on recognizing the difference between guilt and shame."

"There's a difference?"

"Yeah, I guess guilt can be productive. It's like making mistakes and fixing them. Shame makes you feel like a failure—it's not productive."

Rai hummed. "I can see the difference when it's explained that way. Like maybe it's okay to feel guilty if it's something you can fix, but if you can't fix it and it's not productive then it's shame and you need to let it go because it's only hurting you."

"She's got a lot she wants me to do. I'm supposed to come up with a mantra—something concise that I can say to myself to reinforce strength and resiliency. Haven't done that one yet," I huffed and rolled my eyes because having a personal mantra made me feel dumb. "She said we're going to work on challenging negative thoughts. Like if I'm feeling negative I'm supposed to look for the trigger and ask myself what I'm really feeling. Said I'll have to learn to let the unhelpful thoughts go and realize the negative thoughts aren't *me*."

"She talked about Post-It notes," Rai said and kinda huffed. "I guess I'm supposed to stick notes around where I'll see them to give me a boost or something."

I laughed. "That could work. Might feel a little weird." I trailed my hand up and down his arm. "Did she have you make a list of all of your accomplishments and compliments you've gotten? Talk about weird and uncomfortable."

"Yeah, but you gotta admit it felt pretty good to see it when you were done, right?"

I nodded. "Yeah, it did. I think the easiest is telling others thank you. She said that when you show others gratitude it will make them feel positive and inspire the same in you. I feel like I can easily do that one. I have so many people in my life who I'm grateful for."

"Agreed. I like that one. What about volunteering? I think I'd like to do that one. Seeing others in need makes it so it's really hard to feel so negative about yourself or your circumstances."

I nodded. "Yeah, I told her that maybe you and I could find a place to volunteer together." Rai tensed for a split second, but it was enough to let me know that maybe spending more time with me after the whole charade was over wasn't top of his list. "But it probably won't work out with our schedules."

He was quiet for a moment before he whispered, "Yeah. Probably not."

THE SUN PEEKED through the hotel window the next morning and I wanted nothing more than to hold Rai close and pretend our weekend wasn't coming to an end.

Even more, I hated thinking that we likely could stop the fake boyfriends thing in just over a week if Lance and Jerry ended up being together. The cohort dinner would tell us what we needed to know.

"Good morning," Rai murmured, stretching against me.

I kissed the top of his head. "Good morning. You sleep okay? Not too sore?"

"Slept great, why are hotel beds always so much better?"

Because you're in my arms and not alone in your twin bed at home.

"I don't know. Sheets are always top-notch I guess."

Rai rolled on top of me. "If I can be on top, keep things at my pace in case I find out it's too much, can we go again?"

My morning erection was already on-board with the idea, but I didn't want to hurt him. "You'll tell me if it's painful? We can stop and get off another way."

Rai nodded. "I will. I'm not sore now, but I'll stop if it hurts when you're inside."

I reached for the lube as Rai hung over the side of the bed to grab a condom. After rolling the latex down my shaft, I groaned as Rai slicked me with one hand while coating his hole with the other. "You're so damn hot." I gripped his cock and thumbed his leaking slit. "Could get off just like this."

"If it hurts, we'll rub off together, but I want to try this position and we're kinda running out of time." A look of something—was I ridiculous to hope it was sadness?—crossed Rai's face as he shifted farther up my body and reached around to guide my hard length to his entrance.

I gripped Rai's hips, not to push or force, just to hold onto him as he sank his hot, tight ass inch-by-inch on my cock. The urge to thrust up and own his ass was strong, but I bit my lip and groaned, controlling the impulse, as Rai worked himself into a comfortable position.

"Too much?" I asked him when a plaintive cry escaped his lips.

"Just tender. As long as we keep it slow, nothing hard and fast, I think it's okay. Feels amazing this way, the angle is different." Rai wriggled his ass, allowing me to sink the final bit into his heat, and stroked his cock. "I think I liked last night's position better, but this one feels good too." He shifted, his tight heat gripping me as his ass cheeks pressed against my skin. "Can you come like this if you can't pump hard and fast?"

"Not sure, but let's try. If you come first, I can always pull out and jack off on you." In reality, I didn't give a damn how I got off as long as I got to be with Rai.

"Can you touch me?" Rai asked, cheeks pink as he rolled his hips.

I took hold of his cock and began to stroke. "You go slow, I'll go fast." I increased the speed on his shaft as Rai slowly rode my cock.

He moaned and leaned forward to brace his hands on the headboard. "I'm close, Spence. Wanna come."

"Do it, come for me. Want your cum all over me." I jerked his cock, savoring the way he throbbed in my hand. "Wanna watch you come and feel your ass clench around me. Then I'm going to jerk myself until I shoot my load all over you."

Rai whimpered and rode me faster with gentle rolls of his hips. His cock pulsed in my hand, spurting sticky ropes of white up to my chest as the muscles of his ass constricted around me. After a final pulse of his dick, Rai winced and shifted up so my hard dick slid from his body. "Sorry, this probably won't be as good for you."

"I'm gonna get off, nothing not good about it."

"Can I do it for you?" Rai asked, almost shyly.

I shrugged and pulled the condom off. "Do whatever you want, just make me come."

He positioned me much like I'd done to him the night before and put a pillow under my hips. With my legs and ass spread for him, I'd never felt so exposed or vulnerable, but there was no one I trusted more than Rai.

He moved so his mouth was at my ass and reached to grip my dripping cock just as his tongue swirled my rim.

"Fuuuck, Rai." I bucked my hips and fisted the sheets. "Gonna blow in seconds," I warned.

"Do it, wanna know I got you off." Rai continued to stroke me and tongue my ass.

No one has ever gotten me off like you.

In less than a minute, with Rai's tongue teasing my pucker and his fist jerking my cock, I groaned as an orgasm overtook me. I shot my release onto my stomach, my cum mixing with Rai's.

When I caught my breath, I had to fight the urge to pull Rai to me and roll him to his back, smear our jizz between us and just hold him, kiss him, savor him.

Rai quietly rolled from the bed, his back turned to me and his words barely a whisper. "Probably better get ready and pack up, huh?"

The sting of tears threatened my sinuses.

No, I don't want this to end. Let's stay here forever. Why can't this be real?

"Yeah, best to hit the road."

There was no way to stop time and the inevitable would arrive eventually, no matter how badly I wanted to beg the universe for a different outcome.

By that evening, we were back at Remington Place. Back in our shared rooms with the lonely single beds.

We ate an enjoyable dinner with Bev, Dalton, Gabby, and Dre.

Later, Rai begged off of gaming with Dalton and Cooper in favor of homework.

I moped and stewed until Cooper finally convinced me to play.

"Dude, what's wrong with you? You're off or something," Cooper said as he killed my character once again.

"Nothing," I bit out.

Cooper narrowed his eyes at me before throwing a glance toward Dalton. Whether it was some unspoken sibling thing or Dalton just wanted to head to bed, he tossed his controller down and bid us goodnight.

"Okay, now, for real. What the fuck is wrong with you? Something happen with you and Rai this weekend?" Cooper turned off the game.

I scoffed. "Nope. Not at all. Everything going exactly to plan."

"Meaning?"

"Lance seems to be buying we're a couple, looks like he's moved on to a new guy. Can probably call it quits on the whole fake thing and go back to just being friends." I shrugged and studied the controller I still held.

"Why do I get the feeling that maybe you don't want it to end?"

I dropped the controller on the cushion. "Doesn't matter what I want. The plan was clear. Get Lance off Rai's back and then we were done."

Cooper cocked his head. "Did something happen between you two? Like, I know you were figuring you'd have to kiss or something, but did it end up going further?"

"Doesn't. Matter." I stood up and paced the small room. "Said it from the beginning. I'm not his type, he deserves better. I helped him out. Period. End of story."

My best friend, stubborn as always, didn't seem deterred. "But if you *like* him…just want to point out that I *told you* this would happen, but whatever…if you guys like each other, why does it have to end? Just move from fake to real?"

"No. That wasn't what Rai asked for. I'm not

going to put him in a difficult or uncomfortable situation. When it ends, it ends and it will be for the best."

"Then why do your words sound like they're being forced over a cheese grater? Have you even talked to Rai about how he feels?" Cooper crossed his arms and frowned.

"No. Told you, not going to pressure him into something. Things between us have been great, and we'll go back to being friends with no problem. May hurt for a bit, but life sucks and good things never last. Best to remember that." I walked to the window and stared out into the darkness.

"You have to be one of the most obtuse, stubborn men I've ever known. You're lucky I love you." Cooper moved to stand next to me.

"Hey, when Rai and I call it quits, it may be easiest for a while if we're not right on top of each other in that room. Any chance you want to give up your room for good, let Rai take it?"

Cooper winced. "Um, well, about that. I *am* giving up my room."

I cocked a brow. "Really? That's perfect. Rai can have your space. Give us a bit of breathing room as we readjust to just friends." I knew Cooper would go even more ballistic if he knew things between Rai and me had turned sexual so I didn't bring it up.

"Well, the thing is, there's a new guy moving in. He's going to be working for Jesse and Bev's already agreed to let him rent a room." Cooper pursed his lips. "Maybe Cruz—that's the new guy—could take your spot and room with Rai. You could have my old room to yourself? Or I guess Cruz could room with you? He's a bit older than us, think Bev was wanting to give him his own room at least for a while."

The thought of Rai sharing a room with another guy or another guy sleeping across the room from me was enough to make me want to tear my hair out. "No, it's all good. We'll be fine. No reason to mess with what Bev's already got planned." Even though I didn't want to, I forced myself to ask about the new guy. "Cruz? Didn't know Jesse was looking for help."

"Yeah, you know Bev doesn't like us telling too much about the new residents—says they'll tell us about themselves when they're comfortable—but he's new in town, stopped and asked Jesse for work. Jess says he's a kickass mechanic, just hasn't been able to afford all of the certification. Seems like he's moved a lot. Jesse's going to get him on at the Wishing Well part time and give him some hours at the shop. That's why he's coming here, needs something affordable. Seems like a nice guy. Pretty gruff, quiet, maybe has a tough past, but that's just me speculating."

I took a deep breath. "If Bev's okay with him, so am I. She's never misjudged anyone yet. And nowhere better than Remington Place to get a fresh start."

"That's what Jesse and I were thinking." Cooper touched my shoulder. "You sure about this thing with you and Rai ending? I gotta tell you, I think talking to him and letting him know how you're feeling is probably your best bet. Don't let something good slip away because of pride or ignorance."

I just huffed and gave a nod before heading to bed.

Finding Rai curled on his side, his face plastered to a page in a book, study lamp still on, I smiled softly before closing my eyes and forcing away the feeling of longing I had for the guy. We were so damn perfect together—at least in my mind—why couldn't I be brave enough or good enough to offer him more?

I moved the book, turned off the lamp, and pulled the blanket up to Rai's shoulders before leaning in and brushing a kiss over his temple.

ELEVEN
RAI

I'D NEVER BEEN SO DAMN proud as I was to walk into the swanky cohort dinner with Spencer by my side. As much as I adored him in his work boots and worn jeans after a long day on a site, the man was just as drool-worthy in his dress-up duds.

I'd also never been so damn terrified and dreading what I knew was likely coming. Lance had been spouting in class about his new guy, and I'd seen them together at the game shop when I went for an evening of gaming. Spencer would for sure see Lance and Jerry together at the dinner. There'd be no reason for our fake setup to continue and I had absolutely no idea how to stop it from ending.

You could be honest with Spencer and let him know how you feel.

As we took our seats at the assigned table, I pushed the thought away. No, I'd only asked Spencer for this favor because it was temporary. He'd agreed to help me, but he hadn't signed on for me getting attached and wanting more. It wouldn't be fair to switch the details on him now. Bad enough he'd had to give up all this time to fake it with me, I wasn't going to ask for more.

So, you're fine with having sex with him—falling IN LOVE with him—and then just going back to being friends without even having a damn conversation?

I smiled at some classmates as I took a sip of water. Again, the whole *teach me about sex* thing had been agreed to as temporary. It wasn't Spencer's fault I went and fell in love. Wasn't his fault sex with him had ruined me for anyone else. I was stupid enough to get myself into the situation, I had to deal with the consequences.

As the cohort leaders made some speeches, Lance and Jerry walked in looking quite rumpled and it wasn't hard to guess why they were late. Kinda tacky, but whatever.

"Looks like Lance may have finally gotten the clue," Spencer whispered, brushing his lips over my ear as he leaned in.

All I could do was nod.

Emily, one of my favorite teachers, ended her speech at the podium. "Enjoy dinner and we'll reveal the voting results when dessert comes out."

Spencer and I enjoyed friendly chatter with the people at our table, but I knew we were both watching Lance and Jerry. The dinner was delicious —honestly, though, I would have rather been at home with Bev's cooking and our family—and I was stuck in a weird wanting to get out of there and never wanting it to end because I feared what was coming.

As dessert was served, the head of the nursing program took to the microphone to begin the announcements of positions. The cohort had voted on people we thought would be best to serve as our *board* for the rest of our time in the program. The positions were peer-nominated and peer-voted. While I wasn't going to be upset or even shocked if I didn't get a spot, I did really want one because it looked good on a resume.

I smiled and clapped politely as liaisons, treasurer, secretary, and vice president were announced. With each position gone, I saw my chances dwindling, but tried to stay positive. Hopefully, my grades would be enough to help me land a good job upon graduation.

"Our last board position for this year's cohort is president. I have to say that I've never seen this happen, but this person was, of course, nominated by their peers and received a unanimous vote," the head of the program, Vicki, gushed.

Trying not to be obvious, I glanced around trying to figure out who of the remaining members might be named president.

"This year's cohort president is Raiden Ono," Vicki announced.

Unable to believe my ears, I think I blinked multiple times and hopefully didn't let my mouth fall open too far. The hand on my shoulder and warm words at my ear calmed me.

"So damn proud of you," Spencer said gruffly as the diners clapped for me.

Glad that speeches weren't part of the announcements, I tried to give a little smile and appreciative wave to those gathered, but more than likely ended up looking like I'd eaten a mushy banana while offering a weak, flop of my hand.

"New board members, we'll have a meeting next week with the exiting members and get responsibilities and whatnot squared away." Vicki organized her papers. "Now, please feel free to stick around and visit if you'd like."

"You want to stay or go?" Spencer asked me, taking my hand.

"Go? I think I need to get away."

"Let's go." Without another word, my protector —my world—got me out of there and loaded into his truck. "Home?"

I nodded.

"You okay?"

"Yeah, just kinda surprised about the position."

"Proud of you. Always knew you're going to do great things." Spencer merged onto the highway that would get us back to Remington.

"It's an honor. Just wasn't expecting it. Kinda anxious about the extra responsibilities."

"You'll do great. The content and tests already come so easy to you, this will be a drop in the bucket, I'm sure."

When we arrived at home, Spencer turned off the truck but didn't open his door. "Can we talk?"

My stomach hit the floorboard. Here it was. What I'd feared was coming had finally arrived. "Sure."

He took a deep breath. "So, it looked like the plan to get Lance to back off worked, huh?"

I nodded and tried not to grimace. "Yeah, seems like he's moved on. Can't believe he found someone who likes his obnoxious ass, but Jerry looked pretty smitten."

"Guessing you're ready to be done with the whole fake boyfriends thing then, huh?" Spencer didn't look at me, just tapped his thumb on the steering wheel while staring out the windshield. "Ready to move on to bigger and better things?"

No! No, I don't want this to be over. Maybe the fake thing, sure. But I don't want what we have to end. I want it to be real. I'm sorry I roped you into something and then changed the rules, but I love you damn it and I don't want to lose you.

"Yeah, probably for the best." Did Spencer hear the waver in my words?

"That's what I figured," Spencer answered with a hard nod. "So, we'll call it quits and you can be free of me."

"As free as one can be when you're roommates and best friends," I whispered. *The last thing I want is to be free of you, damn it.*

"Well, yeah." He turned a soft smile my way. "It's not like we're saying goodbye for good, just to the boyfriend part."

I blinked to stop the tears. "Yep. And now you can work on real dating maybe. You'll have to run the choices by me for approval, of course." Oh God, I was seriously going to puke. My entire body ached with wanting Spencer to gather me in his arms and tell me this wasn't really happening.

"Same goes for you. Any guy you decide to date will have to pass the Spencer checklist."

Fudge that, Spencer. I don't want to date any other guy. I want you. God, why can't you see that? Why can't I be enough for you?

We climbed from the truck and made our way inside.

I took a quick shower and climbed into bed before Spencer made his way to the bedroom. By the time he emerged from the shower some time later, I had already cried myself to sleep.

A WEEK LATER, I sat in Alicia's office sipping hot tea and eating cookies.

"You want to talk about what's bothering you?" she asked with a kind smile as she tapped her pen on the notebook in her lap.

"Sure. Why not? Maybe you've got some sort of weird, uncomfortable exercise that can help me stop feeling so damn fudging miserable."

Alicia cocked a brow. "We'll see. Give it to me."

"You knew that Spencer and I were pretending to be boyfriends anytime we were around that Lance guy in hopes of him finally getting a clue and moving on, right?"

She nodded.

"Well, what you didn't know was that, until recently, I was a virgin and I asked Spencer to teach me about sex," I huffed out.

I had to give the woman credit, she didn't even flinch. She was good.

"And now our fake boyfriend and sex lessons are done because Lance started dating a guy from the gaming group." I gestured tiredly as if I could brush it all away.

"How are you feeling about all of this?"

"You must have missed the part where I said I was fudging miserable," I bit out. "Sorry."

She nodded and waited.

"I'm miserable. I hate it. I knew the risks going into all of it, but stupid me thought it was worth it and I could deal with the fallout. But I went and fell in love with him and now it hurts so damn bad and I don't know how to fix it," I babbled.

"And Spencer doesn't feel the same?"

I pursed my lips and looked to the floor.

"Raiden? How does Spencer feel?" Alicia pressed.

"He doesn't know. I can't tell him. I promised him the fake thing *and* the sex were all temporary and casual. I can't spring love and shit on him and expect him to be okay with it. I'm not the type of guy Spencer would *ever* go for, he deserves to find his perfect love. Us going back to being friends was the plan from the beginning and I'm not going to dump my emotional baggage on him."

We talked back and forth for several more minutes before Alicia looked at the clock and declared we needed to end for the day.

"Raiden, I can't tell you what to do, but you pay me to give my professional advice. As such, I'm going to advise that you tell Spencer how you're feeling. I have no idea how he'll react, but he deserves your honesty. You and I both know Spencer is working hard to let go of his past and love himself. Finding out his best friend has kept something this huge from him may set his progress back—would likely feed into his notion that no one in his life can be trusted."

I must have given her a horrified look.

"I'm not saying that *you're* responsible for his progress, but I think being honest will be good for both of you." She made a note on the page and gave me a sad smile. "I'll be here for both of you, no matter the outcome."

When I got home, I saw Cooper on the porch with Bev. Hadley was drawing on the driveway with chalk. There was no way to avoid them unless I wanted to be a complete ass, so I plodded up the steps and took a seat next to Bev.

She put an arm around me and pulled me close. Without warning, tears sprang from my eyes and I began to sob.

"Rai, child, what's wrong?" Bev asked, her warm hand rubbing circles on my back.

"I screwed up." I sniffed and wiped at my tears, not wanting to alert Hadley to anything being wrong.

"Mistakes can be fixed," Bev assured.

"Not this one. I think it's too big and it's not just affecting me."

I caught Cooper's eye and he gave me a sad smile. "Spencer?"

I nodded. "I went and fell in love with him. Things went a lot deeper than just fake boyfriends, at least on my part, and now we've moved back to being friends—because that was the plan—and I miss him so damn much."

Cooper nibbled his lip. "And you've told Spencer how you feel?"

I shook my head. "I can't. I don't feel like I can drop that on him when it wasn't what he agreed to."

Bev continued rubbing my back. "Raiden, honest communication is always the best policy. I've been around decades and decades and I can tell you that most problems can be avoided—and solved—with honest communication. I can't make you do anything, you're a grown man and you have to make that decision on your own, but I *can* tell you that I think you're making a monumental mistake—one that will fester and get more painful by the day—if you don't tell Spencer the truth."

I glanced toward Cooper and he nodded. "It's not my place to demand you do something, but I agree that you need to be honest with him. Even if you two never end up as a couple, your friendship depends on you being honest. Don't you think what you and Spencer have is worth honesty, even if it hurts?"

My eyes overflowed with tears again, but I nodded. "I just don't know how to do it; don't know how to handle it when he tells me he can't love me the way I love him."

Bev hummed next to me. "Child, I can't predict the future, but I *can* tell you that the two of you have something special. Whether that's meant to be romantic or platonic, I'm not going to speculate because it's not my place, but I guarantee Spencer loves you in his own special way."

Cooper stood and moved to check on Hadley before returning to the swing—I'd learned that swinging was one of the things that helped keep Cooper calm and focused through his ADHD. "Look, I realize that I was in a very similar situation not too long ago and I was the one being obtuse and stubborn, but I have to tell you, I learned that speaking the truth and dealing with whatever comes of it is the best bet. I was miserable when Jesse and I split up and it didn't get better until we finally told each other the truth." He held a hand up as I began to protest. "I'm not saying that you telling Spencer the truth will end in a happily ever after, I'm just saying that your friendship with the guy deserves the truth."

We sat in comfortable silence for several moments before Hadley told Cooper she was hungry.

"Come on, let's get a snack. We'll be back for dinner once Jesse's done in the shop," Cooper told Bev.

"Cruz is coming to dinner and moving in this weekend, be sure you're here on time. I want everyone to meet him," Bev said.

My head snapped up. "You're giving up your room?"

Cooper smiled and took Hadley's hand. "Yeah, finally stopped being scared and admitted that what Jesse and I have is the real-deal. Someone else needs the space a lot more than me."

AFTER DINNER THAT EVENING, Bev encouraged the adults to go sit on Jesse's patio outside the shop while she and Hadley had a movie night.

Jesse fired up the standing heaters as the entire crew, including our new housemate, settled in. "Good thing it's not full-on winter or it'd be way too cold to sit outside," he said. "Water? Beer? Cider? Soda?"

Instead of letting Jesse serve us, we took turns filing into the shop and grabbing our drinks from the refrigerator. I opted for water since alcohol always made me sleepy and emotional and I was already way too exhausted and emotionally wrung out to deal with any more that night. Plus, I knew Spencer wouldn't drink, so maybe it was a tiny show of support.

As much as I hated the idea of being stuck next to Spencer when I couldn't touch him, I ended up drawn to his side like a damn magnet and sat down in the chair beside him.

"Good to have you with us, Cruz," Spencer said. "Jesse says you're a kick-ass mechanic."

Cruz gave a tiny, shy smile and nodded. "Thanks. Kinda seems crazy that I've got a job and a place to stay after so long of moving around." The man was probably about thirty-five, broad-chested, dark hair and eyes, a scruffy shadow of a beard framing his gorgeous face, and full sleeves of tattoos on both arms. I didn't find myself attracted to him, but I could definitely appreciate a hot guy.

"This is a really great place," Dre said. "You'll like it here. Kinda like a chance to reset yourself."

Cruz rolled the beer bottle between his hands for a moment as he stared at the ground. "I've already told Bev all of this and she said I didn't have to tell all of you. She accepted my request to run a background check and call my references—said I wasn't obligated to share with you anything I didn't want to." He took a deep breath. "But I don't want to start something new with any secrets or lies. I wasn't *in* a gang growing up—hard to believe, I know. Mexican kid, adopted, living near the city, seems like a shoe-in, but my adopted parents did their best to keep me away from the gangs. I made it through high school without much trouble thanks to my parents putting me in a private church school, but after high school—without studies to keep me busy—I fell in with some *friends* I thought would be okay. I ended up in the wrong place at the wrong time with these friends who I found out too late were hanging with the wrong crowd. I ended up arrested and spent five years in prison—probably could have avoided it if we'd had the money for a good lawyer, but we didn't. I've been out eight years, have a clean record—Bev called my old parole officer; haven't had to check in with him in well over three years—but I've been from place to place trying to get a job, settle down. Not a lot of people give an ex-con a chance." Cruz took a long breath and let it out slowly. "I'm telling you all of this because I need to know you're all okay with me being here. If not, I understand and I'll move on, no hard feelings. I can't try to start over if the people in my house are scared or uncomfortable."

Dalton took Gabby's hand. "No issues here. We trust Bev with our lives and we know she's a good judge of character. If she's welcomed you in, we welcome you in."

Dre nodded and gestured toward Cruz with his can. "Same. I think all of us have some shit in our past, maybe we're running from it. Maybe we're just looking for that chance to start over. My aunt knows good people and potential when she sees it. Got no problem with you being here."

Cooper took Jesse's hand. "If Jesse and Bev both trust you, I'm good. Everyone deserves a chance."

Fighting the urge to grab Spencer's hand, I gave Cruz a smile. "As the newest housemate before you, I can tell you that this place is amazing and if you passed Bev's test, you're fine by me."

Spencer cleared his throat. "I know what it's like

to have your past haunting you. Welcome to Remington Place."

A look of relief washed over Cruz's face and we settled in to chatting about our jobs and hobbies.

"So, let me get this straight," Cruz said. "Dalton and Gabby share a room. Cooper used to live here, but moved in with Jesse. Spencer and Rai are roomies." Yeah, punch me in the gut why don't ya? "Dre has an opening in his room?"

We all nodded.

"Your room *could* be a double, but it's set to be a single for now," Cooper explained.

"Yeah, Bev said she'd leave it a single unless an emergency situation arose after Dre ended up with a roommate," Cruz said.

By the time our little crew broke up—it was nice having such a spread of ages from me and Cooper at twenty-five all the way up to Jesse at fifty-ish, yet still able to visit and laugh and call each other friends—I was convinced that Cruz was going to be good for the house and I was glad he'd found us. He looked sad and lonely, but spending time at Remington Place would hopefully remedy that.

I couldn't help but wonder why he was so sad? Spending time in prison couldn't have been easy. Moving place to place likely meant he had no real connections or relationships. Did he have family around?

I swallowed hard as I gave Cruz a smile before heading to my room. I didn't want to spend my life sad and alone. Talking to Spencer, telling him how I really felt, wouldn't automatically make the pain go away, but maybe it would help get me on the path to healing—one way or the other.

TWELVE

SPENCER

"ANYTHING YOU'D LIKE to talk about today?" Alicia said as our session began.

I shrugged and stared into my mug of tea.

As per her usual, she waited patiently until words started to pour from of me. I'd learned quickly in our sessions that she'd eventually get me to talk and I'd feel better—which shocked me—so I usually talked sooner rather than later these days. But I liked to pretend I was in control of the situation.

"You know how Rai and I were pretending to date so that Lance guy would leave him alone?" Every time I talked about our little situation, it sounded ridiculous, but I couldn't regret the time spent with Rai, even if it had been fake.

Alicia nodded and sipped her tea.

"Well, the goal was met. Lance started dating

some other guy, so we called it quits." My stomach rolled and I couldn't even think of taking a bite of a cookie.

"And how are you feeling about that?" Alicia made a note on her paper.

I took a drink of tea and then stared at the floor for a long time. "It sucks."

"Why's that?"

Placing my mug onto the little coffee table, I flopped back against the couch with a sigh. "Because things got pretty hot and heavy between us and nothing we did was fake, at least not on my end."

Alicia stared at me. "Go on."

I ran my hands through my hair. "We went a lot further than just faking a relationship and I think my dumb ass went and fell in love with him."

"And how does Raiden feel about that?" She made another note.

Grunting, I rested my arm over my eyes.

"Have you told Rai how you feel?"

I shook my head.

"Why not?"

Sitting up, leaning my elbows on my knees, I held my head in my hands. "Because he asked me for a favor, he didn't ask me to fall in love with him."

"Is that it?"

"And," I blew out a deep breath, "I *want* to be the right guy for him, but that little voice keeps whispering that he could do so much better than me."

"What is it about you that you wish was *better*?"

I scoffed. "What is there that I *don't* wish was better? I grew up poor in a shitty house with a shitty mom in a shitty situation. Never had nice things, never had the good stuff happen, could never trust anyone."

"Okay, all of those things are in the past. What is it about Spencer in the here and now that needs to be *better* for Rai? Or for anyone?"

"Don't want just *anyone*," I gritted out, but I answered her question. "I'm a construction worker. I live in shared housing, drive an older truck, have no family, and can't measure up to Rai's potential."

Alicia scribbled on her paper. "Let's start with the family. Has Rai indicated he needs a partner to have blood family in order to be with him?"

I rolled my eyes. "No."

"You and he both have a very solid, supportive chosen family, yes?"

I nodded.

"Okay, your truck. Is Rai the type of person who appears to need the newest, shiniest, most expensive vehicle to make him happy?"

Snorting out a laugh, I thought of his little green clunker. "No."

"Shared housing? Are you living there because you can't afford elsewhere or for some other reason?"

I shrugged. "Started out because I couldn't afford elsewhere. Now, it's because my friends and family are there." I bit my lip. "I've got money saved to build my own place, but it seems dumb to move away from Remington Place just to build a lonely house for myself."

"Do you look down on Rai for living in shared housing?"

I frowned. "Of course not."

"You spoke of Rai's potential and yours not measuring up. Tell me more about that."

I closed my eyes and pinched the bridge of my nose. "Rai is going to be this amazing nurse. Helping people, caring for them, saving them, he's going to do it all and be damn good at it. Me? I build houses. What's so great about that?"

Alicia made a note as she nodded her head. "You're a construction worker; you've told me you work on various aspects of a building project from start to finish. Correct?"

I nodded.

"From what you told me a few sessions ago, it

sounds like you're building a name for yourself if that guy at the convention knew you." Alicia raised a brow.

I huffed, a brief jag of pride still cutting through me, "Probably didn't mean anything. They're basically head-hunters, they have to know their stuff."

"Tell me again some of the houses and buildings you've worked on around the area. The ones you're the most proud of."

Narrowing my eyes at her, I took a breath and played her game. "Children's wing at that hospital in Madden. Homeless shelter on the boarder of Remington and Wilmington. Low-income subdivision in Remington. Food pantries in Remington and Prestwood. Habitat for Humanity homes in Madden, Remington, and Prestwood."

"And why do those projects bring you the most pride?"

"They're not just to sell and make money, they're there to help people," I answered, raising and lowering one shoulder.

"All great in their own right. What about the regular ol' houses you've built? What are they good for?" Alicia doodled on her page.

I pursed my lips. "I mean, some of the bigger, richer areas kinda seem like overkill and more luxury than just basic shelter, but the other homes—especially the ones that we've gone in and done repairs on—they're good for providing safe shelter for the residents."

"So, you'd agree, that no matter what projects you've been involved in, every single one of them—even the most luxurious—have *something* good about them? Maybe they provide shelter? Protection? Food? A safe place? A chance to start over?"

I took a deep breath and let it out slowly. "Yeah, but not because it's *me* working on them. Anyone could do what I do, I'm nothing special."

Alicia shook her head. "Inaccurate. That's one of those things I need you to question when you think it. Could *anyone* truly do what you do? Could I? Could Rai?"

"Well, I mean, with training…"

"No, just like you couldn't do my job or ace one of Rai's tests—not because you're not *capable*, but because you don't have the learned skills—not just *anyone* could do what you do. Those buildings, the children's wings, those homes, the repairs, all of them are providing someone—individuals and families—with basic needs and it's because of *your* skill, *your* hard work."

I huffed. "I get what you're saying, but

construction workers are a dime a dozen. If I quit, they'd replace me within a day."

Alicia nodded. "Therapists are pretty plentiful as well. Do you think if I quit and you found someone new…" she paused and chuckled at the look of fear on my face, "…that you could just start up with the new person and get exactly what you get with me?"

"No." I shook my head.

"Don't get me wrong. My point isn't that there aren't other good therapists or construction workers or waiters or nurses out there. My point is that no one can do your job exactly like you because they aren't *you*." Alicia twirled her pen. "You bring something unique to every project, every conversation, every relationship."

I closed my eyes and tried to believe her.

"And I think Rai deserves a few things," she said quietly after a few moments.

My eyes flew open and I waited.

"First," she held up her index finger, "he deserves the truth. It's not fair of you to keep it from him. Whether he feels the same or not, you owe it to him, to your friendship, to be honest with him."

Nodding, I knew deep down that she was right.

"Two," she put up another finger, "he deserves to make his own decision on what he deserves. He's your friend, he knows the uniqueness you bring to life, and he should be allowed to decide what that means for him." She smiled softly. "And three," up popped a third finger, "he deserves to be trusted. If he decides he loves you right back, trust that he's capable of knowing how he feels. If he says friendship is all he wants, trust that he's weighed the decision. Trust that he loves you as a friend and wants to keep that."

We sat quietly for a few moments until I finally took a deep breath and planted my hands on my knees. "That's all well and good—gotta say, I'm fucking terrified of how to make the just friends thing work if that's what he decides—but there's one big problem."

Alicia cocked an eyebrow.

"I have absolutely no idea how to bring this up to Rai. When and where is the right time to tell your best friend that you've fallen in love with him and you want more than just a shared room and friendship?" Just the thought of it had my heart nearly pounding out of my chest.

"In this case, my advice is to just rip the band-aid off. Don't wait, don't sugar coat it, just tell him." Alicia made a final note on her notebook before closing it and glancing at the clock. "Depending on the outcome, ripping it off may be scary and it may hurt, but you can either start really living instead of hiding or you can start healing. Either way, you and Rai both deserve the truth."

ALICIA'S WORDS were still heavy in my mind as I helped Cruz carry in some boxes the next day. Rai had been busy with work and school and his new board president gig so I hadn't seen much of him. It sucked to not see him, sucked to think he was maybe avoiding me, sucked that I wanted so badly to see him, everything just sucked donkey balls.

"So, you and Rai, huh?" Cruz asked as we dropped the boxes on his bedroom floor.

"Huh? Oh, um, no."

Cruz cocked his head. "Really? Thought I got a vibe."

"Oh, you mean gay? Yeah, we're both gay." I stood a little straighter and wondered if I needed to prepare for an issue. "That a problem?"

Cruz held up his hands in front of his chest. "Not at all. Kinda a relief. Knew I was gay from the time I was a kid. Never acted on it or came out—church school and highly religious parents didn't lend to that type thing, ya know?" He shrugged. "Then I ended up in prison, parents died, haven't ever been somewhere longer than a month or so." Cruz slipped his hands in his pockets. "Moving around so much doesn't exactly make for easy relationships. Always kinda felt like survival was more important than finding someone to fuck, ya know?"

"So, you've never had sex?" I couldn't help the surprise.

"Nah, I kept up appearances in high school. Didn't date a lot, but enough to never get questioned. Bad enough to be the only brown-skinned guy in the Catholic school, didn't need all the jocks getting any idea that I might be gay."

I nodded. "I can see that."

"So, really, you and Rai aren't a thing?" Cruz cocked his head.

Grinding my teeth, I gritted out, "It's complicated. Why? You interested?"

Cruz laughed. "Nah, man. He's cute as hell, but I don't butt in where I'm not wanted. You can tell me it's complicated all you want, but I saw the way you two looked at each other. I may be a virgin when it comes to sex with a man, but I've got eyes and I can see when two guys are hot for each other." He opened a box. "Maybe you two should uncomplicate things? No reason to be mopey and miserable if the situation is fixable." He dropped his chin to his chest. "Sorry, man, not really my place to come in and start doling out advice." With a shrug and a shy smile, he went on. "Just feeling damn good to be somewhere safe, somewhere I can maybe build some friendships. See two people looking as sad as you two do when you're around each other, just makes sense to want you to fix it. *I* may be sad and alone, but that doesn't mean I want the people around me to suffer the same fate."

I stared at him for a moment before giving a quick nod and darting from the room. Rai looked at me like he was hot for me? Surely Cruz was reading things wrong. Right?

Whether Cruz was onto something or not, Alicia was right. I needed to tell Rai how I felt. Living suspended in misery and the unknown was eating at me. If, after I told him everything, Rai still said he could only do friends, I'd have my answer and be free to move forward with my future.

THIRTEEN
RAI

"DINNER WILL BE ready in about an hour," Bev told me as I came in from class and work.

"Okay, thanks."

"You boys ever gonna talk it out and quit the moping?" Bev asked, stirring whatever smelled delicious on the stove.

I took a deep breath. "Yeah, I'm going to talk to him now. Hopefully."

Bev glanced over her shoulder. "Well, missing dinner isn't an option. So, whether the conversation goes well or crashes hard, I expect you both down here to eat."

Smiling, I hitched my backpack on my shoulder and gave a salute. "Wouldn't dream of missing dinner." I took the stairs to our room and prayed I wouldn't hyperventilate.

Spencer, spread out on his bed, glanced up from his phone.

"You get off early today?" I dropped my bag on the floor.

"Yeah, rain washed us out. Go in early tomorrow to try to get caught up." He tossed his phone to the side. "How was class? Work?"

I loved that he always truly seemed to want to hear about my day.

"Class was good. Spent a lot of time on the pediatric unit today, there's so much to learn. Work was busy, good tips, but I'm exhausted." Pacing with nervous energy, I tried to decide if I should sit or stand.

"You given any thought to what type of nursing you want to do? Emergency? Pediatric? Hospital? Office? Seems like there are tons of options, yeah?"

I nodded. "Haven't really decided on a specific area yet. May just depend on what job I can get after graduation and then go from there." Wiping my hands on my jeans, I bit my lip.

"You okay? You seem nervous." Spencer sat up.

"Yeah, I'm good. Just wondering if you had a bit to talk."

"Always," he patted the bed beside him.

Wondering if I was stupid to sit so close with all I needed to say, I went ahead and settled in next to him. "I have a lot I need to say and I kinda need you to just listen while I get it all out and then we can talk about it." I chewed the corner of my lip. "If that's okay?"

Spencer looked like I'd just told him I had terrible news, but he nodded. "Yeah, that's good. We should probably talk."

"I've had a thing for you since the first time you came in the diner," I blurted. "Our friendship, your support, all of it means everything to me." I pulled my knee under me and a bit toward him. "Then I got stupid and selfish."

Spencer started to protest, but I stopped him.

"I knew what I was doing," I sighed, closing my eyes to the pain. "From the very beginning, I *knew* there was no way you'd go for a guy like me. I figured my only chance with you was to play up the friend thing and ask for help. I knew it was dumb. I knew I risked making you angry, losing you, getting hurt." I wrapped my arms around myself. "The craving I had for you made me do foolish things, but I will *never* regret what we had together, even if it was just you helping me out, I need you to know that. I'm not a stupid person, but I stupidly let lust overtake me; I thought I could get everything I wanted with you, get it out of my system, close the door on it because *you* weren't interested, and that would be the end of it." I ran my hand through my hair. "I wasn't prepared for being steamrolled by all these feelings. Instead of getting you out of my system and moving on, you ended up cemented into my heart and I don't know how to even fathom being with someone else." I held up my hands to stop Spencer's words. "I get it. I know I'm not the one for you. I've known it from the beginning. Hindsight is twenty-twenty, but at the time, I wasn't counting on the gentleness of your kisses. Wasn't planning on how quickly your touch would set me on fire, consume me so completely. I went into our little fake relationship thinking I'd get to experience something I've never had before with someone I trusted. I came out of it realizing that what we had is something I very likely will never find again." I paused and glanced up at Spencer. "You're it for me, Spence. The person I trust, the person I love, the person I want to spend the rest of my life with." Closing my eyes against the pain, I whispered, "I'm sorry to put you in this position, but I needed you to know everything— why I did it, where it went wrong, how I feel. I know it's not fair to you, but keeping it hidden was eating at me and wasn't fair either." Taking a deep, shuddering breath, I croaked, "I'm going to talk to Bev about possibly rearranging some sleeping quarters. Figure we could maybe do with a bit of separation."

"Stop," Spencer bit out. "Look, you said your words and now it's my turn. It took two people to put us in this situation." He took a deep breath and shook his head. "I kept telling myself—even while my head was screaming at me that it was a bad idea —that I could do the fake thing—even the sex—and not get in too deep. It should have been easy. Help a friend then move on. I don't think I'm the right person for you; you deserve so much more than me. I should have been able to stick to that."

I tried to argue that, but Spencer stopped me.

"I told myself I'd help you out *as your friend* and only because I wanted you to be safe. But in reality, I'm a selfish, greedy bastard and I knew that the time we spent together was the only way I'd ever allow myself to be with you." He took my face in his hands. "Don't you *ever* think it was because I don't like you or don't find you attractive. In a different world, if I could have turned out better, I would pick you time and time again."

Taking a shaky breath, I leaned into Spencer's touch.

"The thought of kissing you, touching you, being inside you, sharing all of what we shared, and then sending you off to do it *for real* with someone else nearly killed me. But I kept telling myself that it was my best chance of keeping you safe, even if I wanted to rip off someone's face every time I thought of another person touching you."

"I don't want anyone else to touch me," I whispered, tears stinging my sinuses.

Spencer caressed my cheeks with his thumbs. "I didn't mean to. I didn't *want* to. In fact, I fought it so hard I nearly gave myself a nervous breakdown." His deep brown eyes searched mine. "It was supposed to be fake and temporary. Then I'd let you go and watch as my *friend* spread his wings and moved on." He shook his head. "But I lost myself in you. All of what we did was supposed to be fake and practice to make it look real for getting Lance off your back, but I let myself imagine it was real. Let myself believe you could really respond to my kisses and touches that way. Let myself believe you could maybe someday curl into my arms and let me hold you." Spencer closed his eyes. "I know it's not fair to you and I know I have no right. I don't even know how it happened because I didn't think I knew how to, but I went and fell in love with you. I know I have to let you go…"

A crazed laugh bubbled from my lips as hope

spread warm and gooey in my chest. "Stop it," I ordered, putting my finger to his mouth, a hot tear rolling down my cheek. "Did you not hear what I said? I *love* you. If you love me, I don't see how this is a problem."

"You deserve so much better…"

"I swear, if you say that one more time, I may throat punch you. *I* deserve to be safe, happy, and loved. Would you agree?" I asked.

Spencer nodded.

"Who is always protecting me and keeping me safe? Hell, who agreed to a crazy fake relationship just to keep me safe?" I raised my brow and waited for his answer.

"Me," Spencer muttered.

"Who makes me laugh? Who lets me read bedtime stories to him? Who goes out of his way to keep me happy, but is also right there to hold me when I'm sad?"

Spencer huffed. "Me, but…"

"No buts. Who loves me?"

"I do," Spencer whispered. "But you're going to be so damn successful in your future, you don't need me holding you back."

"*You* are already damn successful. There is nothing about building homes to be ashamed of. Hell, maybe someday we'll take our little duo on the road and journey near and far building safe housing and providing basic medical care." I wrapped my arms around his waist. "My point is, we didn't plan on it, neither of us thought it was a good idea or possible, but we went and fell in love with each other. I think we owe it to ourselves to at least see how it plays out." My head was spinning from the conversation; never in my wildest dreams had I thought to hope that Spencer could love me back.

"I thought you were going to ask Bev for a new room?" Spencer smirked.

I shrugged. "That was before I realized the hot-as-sin, caring, supportive, amazing-in-bed guy I fell in love with loves me right back."

His lips brushed mine. "I do. So much." He pulled away enough to speak. "I have *a lot* of things to work through and fix."

"Do you remember what I told you about wabi-sabi? We each have permission to be our true self. We have to learn to embrace the perfection of being imperfect, see the good in our messiness."

"I want better for *you*."

"You *are* my better. I wish you could see yourself the way I see you." I pulled a piece of paper from my pocket. "I've been carrying this around for a while. Wanting to share it with you, but not sure of when." I handed it to him.

Spencer took the paper with shaking hands.

"Read it. Out loud." I tipped his chin and brushed a kiss over his lips. "Please."

He unfolded the paper and cleared his throat before beginning to read. "Come to me whole, with your flaws, your scars, and everything you consider imperfect. Then let me show you what I see. I see galaxies in your eyes and fire in your hair. I see journeys in your palms and adventures waiting in your smile." Spencer's voice cracked and he sniffed. "I see what you cannot: You are absolutely, maddeningly, irrevocably perfect. Ariana Dancu." He drew in a deep, shaky breath and blew it out slowly.

"I heard a piece of that quote during a meditation Alicia had me doing. I looked it up and it punched me in the gut. It's exactly how I see you." I ran a thumb along his scruffy jaw.

Spencer pulled me close, wrapping me tightly in his arms and pressing a kiss against my head as he breathed in deeply. "I love you so damn much. I can't see myself that way. Not yet, but I'll keep working on it."

"Can you let me love you enough for both of us for now?" I kissed the stubbled skin of his cheek.

"As long as you let me do my very best to love you the way you deserve to be loved," he whispered as he tipped my chin. "I love you."

"Imperfections and all," I murmured. "I love you, too."

His mouth met mine, sealing our promises with warm, wet lips and tongues.

"Dinner will be ready soon." I couldn't bring myself to pull away from the kiss more than to murmur against his lips.

"We can continue this later. After all, we have the whole room." Spencer nipped at my lip. "But I have something for you."

My eyes went wide. "A present? I didn't get you anything."

"You gave me you, that's plenty," Spencer said with a chuckle as he dug around in his dresser and pulled out a little bag. "It's not a big deal. I figured I was being ridiculous buying it when we were supposed to be faking everything." He stepped close and cupped my face. "But I need you to know, there was *never* a time when anything we did or said was fake on my part. I may have pretended to be pretending—which, yeah, sounds really weird—but every kiss, every touch, every word was real and true."

With my heart floating like a damn helium balloon, I took the bag he held out.

I reached in and pulled out a miniature snow globe with *Midwest Snow* and the year on the outside and two skiing figures surrounded by floating snow and hearts on the inside. Tears stung my eyes.

"You said you weren't much for souvenirs, and even though it was supposed to be fake, I couldn't help but want to remember our time together," Spencer said with a shrug.

"I love it," I choked out and plastered my mouth to his in a searing kiss that promised so much more. "I love *you*."

Spencer, eyes suspiciously bright, cleared his throat. "I still don't understand why, but..."

I cocked my brow, just waiting for him to put himself down.

"...but I'll allow it because I love you, too. So damn much." He kissed me again and hugged me close.

"Boys, dinner is ready," Bev's voice traveled up the stairs.

"She threatened me with bodily harm if we missed dinner," I whispered against Spencer's lips.

"Dinner first. Later, I've got plans for you." Spencer swatted at my ass as we headed downstairs.

The entire crew glanced up as we thundered down the stairs.

There must have been something on our faces, because everyone except Hadley smirked, smiled, or laughed as Spencer and I took our places at the table.

"What?" Spencer groused.

"Guess it's not so complicated," Cruz said with a shy smile as he handed a bowl of potatoes to his left.

Spencer's cheeks pinked. "Fine, all of you who kept saying Rai and I needed to talk to each other, I finally took your advice and it ends up you were right."

I chuckled. "Funny, that was the same advice they were giving me." I elbowed him. "And if I'm remembering correctly, I started the conversation."

"Yeah, but that's because you're the academic and I'm somewhat stunted in the area of doing what's best for me," Spencer said as he leaned over and kissed my cheek.

"Hallelujah," Bev mumbled. "'Bout time you two got that worked out. We need some time without drama around here."

"We're sorry for causing drama," Spencer said.

"Child, I'm just playin'. As long as it's harmless—especially if it ends in happiness—I say bring it on. You children keep me young and entertained. Now," Bev demanded, "pass the food before it gets cold. I didn't bust my butt cooking to see it go to waste."

While the food made its way around the table, Cooper leaned over and whispered. "You guys are good? You're for real this time?"

Spencer took my hand and we both smiled. "Not

that it was ever truly fake, but yeah, it's for real." He kissed my knuckles.

"For real and forever, if I have anything to say about it," I added.

Spencer shrugged. "You know I can't say no to you."

EPILOGUE

SPENCER

Three months later

"You want to go get that ice cream, or you want to take advantage of an empty house?" I nuzzled Rai's neck. "Everyone is gone for about thirty more minutes."

Rai pretended to consider his options. "Well, I really do want ice cream…"

I cut him off by rolling him to his back and covering his body with mine before devouring his mouth. Kissing Rai never got old and when he sucked on my tongue and rocked his hips, I knew ice cream could wait.

We'd gone out and purchased a queen bed the day after we talked and put both twin beds in the basement storage. The entire house knew we were having sex—and lots of it—but we did our best to keep it quiet and took advantage of the rare occasions when everyone was gone.

"Get the lube," Rai demanded as he sat up and yanked his shirt over his head before shimmying out of his pants and boxers.

Rai had set appointments for us to get tested just a few days after we made everything official and we'd been having sex without condoms since then. Never in a million years had I thought I'd find someone to love and trust the way I did Rai, but I was beginning to accept that maybe I *did* deserve all the good in my life.

"Get naked," Rai urged. "We can be as loud and dirty as we want."

I chuckled and stripped. A lot of our sex was as quiet as possible—still hot, sweaty, and fucking unbelievable, just quiet—so an empty house was a cause for celebration.

"Does my noisy little minx want me to fudge him hard and fast?" I teased.

Rai stuck out his tongue. "No. Your noisy boyfriend wants you to drill him into the mattress and make him scream."

My hard cock was immediately on board with that request and I slicked myself as Rai rolled to his stomach.

"Get up on your knees," I said, gripping his hips and pulling him up.

With Rai's ass spread for me, I leaned in and swirled my tongue against his hole, loving the way he moaned my name. I spent several moments tonguing his rim, working him open, and making him writhe at my touch before spreading lube around his pucker and pressing a finger inside.

"God, yes, so good. Do two and then get inside me. Need to feel you," Rai panted through his words.

When I was sure he was stretched enough, I pressed his body to the mattress and straddled his thighs. Shifting into the right position, I worked my cock between his cheeks and groaned at the slick heat that awaited me. Lining up my throbbing dick with Rai's hole, I pushed in slowly as he whimpered with each inch I gave him. Once I was fully sheathed in his tight heat, I braced on my arms and began the hard and fast thrusting Rai begged for.

"Shit, Spence, oh shit. So good. Fudge, harder, harder. Oh God, feels so good," he babbled, his fists gripping the sheets.

"You gonna come?" I asked between gritted teeth. Hard and slow, I could last for quite a while. Hard and fast, I was lucky if I didn't blow within seconds.

"Come in me then suck me off," Rai begged.

I smiled as I continued to pummel his ass. Rai loved a good pounding, but he also never got tired of feeding me his cock and coming down my throat. I was always happy to oblige. Picking up the pace, I thrust harder and faster until Rai was crying out my name. With a final push of my hips, my cock exploded in his heat, pulse after pulse of my release filling him.

Dropping to press my chest against his back, I kissed his neck and whispered, "So fucking good. Love you so much. You okay?"

"Mmhm, love you, too," Rai murmured. "I'll be better when my cock is in your throat."

"Such a dirty talker for someone who can't say *fuck*," I teased as I slipped from his body and rolled him to his back.

"Shut up and suck me," Rai ordered, fisting his cock and pressing the leaking head against my lips.

I obeyed his command and swallowed him deep as I cupped his balls before moving to dip two fingers into his dripping hole.

"Oh, shit," Rai cried out. "Yeah, love that. Oh, damn."

I loved to hear my guy babble and whimper at my touch.

Working his cock with one hand and my mouth, and his hole with my fingers, I sucked and thrust, my touch brushing his gland, until he threw his head back and groaned my name. His salty, bitter release coated my tongue as his ass clenched around my fingers. I slipped my fingers from his body and let his spent dick fall from my mouth as he came down from his high and caught his breath.

A door downstairs slammed.

"Perfect timing," I said with a laugh.

"Or, they walked in and heard all the noise we were making and decided to slam the door so we'd know they were here." Rai threw an arm over his eyes, panting.

"Eh, that was so good, I don't even care if they heard us." I pressed soft kisses up his body until I reached his mouth. Kissing him slowly, sharing his flavor with him as our tongues danced together, I gathered him in my arms. "Love you."

"Love me enough to take me for ice cream now?" Rai raised a brow.

"We really should shower, but it's your ass that will be dripping cum, not mine." I shrugged. "You want ice cream right now?"

He nodded. "I'll clean up real quick. We can shower later. Together."

"Never can say no to you." I rolled from bed and used a towel to clean myself.

Once we'd both washed up and gotten dressed, we headed out for ice cream.

I laughed when my phone buzzed while waiting in line because I *knew* it was Rai sending me ten dollars for the ice cream.

Gathering his plain vanilla and my cookies-n-cream, I met him on the sidewalk and kissed him before handing him his cone. We walked a couple blocks to where I'd parked and climbed in to head back to Remington Place.

"You know, Bev will be pissed if we ruin our dinner," Rai said as we walked from the truck toward the house.

"We didn't get the big cones and it's still a couple hours until mealtime, I think we can pull it off." I glanced at a car I didn't recognize in front of the house. "Wonder who's here."

As we walked up the back steps, raised voices floated on the air.

Rai and I both frowned. Remington Place wasn't known for raised voices.

Entering the kitchen, I took in that almost the whole gang was there, plus one new guy I didn't recognize although he looked familiar for some reason. Tall, broad-shouldered, coppery brown skin, dark hair in an extra short fade, and striking blue eyes.

"Ms. Bev, I can switch rooms," Cruz said quietly.

"You'll do no such thing. I have rules in this house for a reason. The reasons may be mine and mine alone, but I have the final say." Bev placed a calming hand on Cruz's arm. "You were the last to move in, you'll be the last to get a roommate." She turned fiery eyes toward Dre and the new guy and pointed a finger. "As for you two, you'll figure yourselves out and show some respect in this house. I don't know your history—the good Lord knows there seems to be a mighty one—but you'll pay your rent, abide by my rules, and leave the drama out of it."

"But, Aunt Bev," Dre groaned.

The new guy bristled. "Ma'am, I'm mighty appreciative of the room. Dre and I do have a bit of a history. Maybe if you and I could speak in private?"

"Nonsense, there are no secrets in this house, Khi," Bev answered.

"Right." The new guy, Khi, nodded and turned to Dre. "Man, this isn't what I want either, but I'm desperate for a place to stay and knowing my sister is here makes it even better. Can we please just choose to ignore each other. I'll do my best to stay out of your way and you show me the same respect."

Ahhh, Khi was Gabby's brother. No wonder he looked familiar.

Gabby hooked her arm through Khi's. "Come on, you can unpack and then we can catch up." She shot Dre a look that dared him to say differently.

Dre sighed. "Fine. I'm not home that much anyway. We'll stay out of each other's way."

Khi and Dre gave each other curt nods before Gabby led Khi upstairs.

Bev crossed her arms and glared at her nephew. "You want to tell me what that was about?"

Dre huffed. "Not really. We went to the same high school. He was a senior, I was a freshman. Never saw eye-to-eye. We were in some of the same sports and groups. Not really my place to tell his side of things, but suffice it to say there's never been any love lost between us."

Bev studied him for a moment. "Fine line between love and hate," she muttered before glancing at Rai and me. "Guess it's a good thing you two got your acts together since it looks like these two yahoos are bringing their own drama."

Rai and I just smiled and ate our ice cream. I prayed Bev was so wrapped up in Dre and Khi that she wouldn't recognize we were eating sugar before dinner. No way I wanted her wrath turned our way.

"Aunt Bev, no drama. I swear. I've got my fashion work and full-time job on the ambulance. I'm sure Khi will be busy with his job; I mean, he moved to

Remington just for the job, right? We'll probably barely see each other."

"Mmhm," Bev hummed before turning a critical eye toward Cruz. "You have any drama you're planning on bringing to my doorstep?" She spoke harshly, but I knew she wasn't truly mad.

Cruz held up his hands. "No, ma'am. No drama here. Had enough of that to last a lifetime." He made the sign of the cross. "Just happy to have some stable, paying jobs, a bed, food, and good friends. Not looking for any kind of trouble."

Bev made a clucking noise. "Better hope trouble doesn't find *you*."

THE END

Want more of the Remington Place crew? Look for Desire and Yearn on your favorite book platform. Buying direct from the author is always an appreciated option https://payhip.com/ ADEllisAuthor

NOTES

If you'd like to learn more about Wabi Sabi, please find information here-

https://nakamotoforestry.com/japanese-culture-the-actual-meaning-of-wabi-sabi/

https://www.utne.com/mind-and-body/wabi-sabi

ALSO BY A.D. ELLIS

Find all of A.D. Ellis's books at https://books2read.com/ap/RWrrNx/AD-Ellis

The **Remington Place** series continues - <u>Desire</u> (book 3) is a steamy, age-gap, hurt/comfort M/M romance featuring a heart-of-gold mechanic and a twink who's a lot stronger than he realizes. *Please note: This story has mention of sex trafficking and sexual abuse.*

<u>Power Struggle</u> is a steamy M/M, age-gap, forced proximity romance set in a small town. A twenty-year history, rival schools and jobs, and a hotel with only one bed make for a hot and heavy, sweet and sexy, HEA-guaranteed love story.

<u>Take Me Home</u> M/M age-gap, opposites-attract romance with plenty of steam and a scene that will make you appreciate camouflage and work boots

<u>Let Love In</u> M/M age-gap, forced proximity, dad's best friend, bisexual-awakening romance. Available on AUDIO!

<u>Let Love Win</u> M/M brother's best friend romance. Available on AUDIO!

<u>Buried Secrets</u> Romantic suspense stand-alone title. Available on AUDIO!

<u>Silver in the City</u> (3 books- meet the Silver crew you read about in Forged in the City) Available on AUDIO!

<u>Forged in the City</u> (3 books- a spin-off series from Silver in the City) Available on AUDIO

<u>The BJ Boys Series</u> (3 books, small town, big love) Available on AUDIO

<u>Forever Better Together</u> (friends to lovers) Available on AUDIO!

<u>His Reluctant Cowboy</u> (age gap, opposites attract, cowboy romance) Available on AUDIO!

<u>What Blooms Beneath</u> (LGBT Fantasy romance) Available on AUDIO!

<u>Sawyer</u>

(this was the first M/M I wrote and you may remember Sawyer and Luke being mentioned in <u>Barrett & Ivan</u> as well as in <u>Ryker & Gavin</u>)

ACKNOWLEDGMENTS

It's always so hard to write this part because I'm worried I'll forget someone without meaning to.

Readers- you are the reason I write. As long as you continue reading my stories, I'll continue writing them. Thank you for your support.

Bloggers- your support, reviews, and promotion are very much appreciated. Thank you!

My author buddies- I don't know that I could keep doing this without our brainstorm sessions, laughter, road trips, meals, wine, and friendship as my support.

Thank you to my alphas, betas, editors, proofreaders, and ARC readers! Your eyes and input are beyond important to me.

Brett and Gage- as usual, I doubt you even grasp how much your support, input, and friendship mean to me. This author journey has brought many wonderful things into my life, and you both are two of the BEST! I'm blessed to call you friends.

My family and friends- thank you for your love and support, always.

ABOUT THE AUTHOR

A.D. Ellis is an Indiana girl, born and raised. She spends much of her time in central Indiana as an instructional coach/teacher in the inner city of Indianapolis, being a mom to two amazing older teens children, and wondering how she and her husband of almost two decades have managed to not drive each other insane. A lot of her time is also devoted to phone call avoidance and her hatred of cooking.

She loves chocolate, wine, pizza, and naps along with reading and writing romance. These loves don't leave much time for housework, much to the chagrin of her husband. Who would pick cleaning the house over a nap or a good book? She uses any extra time to increase her fluency in sarcasm.

Find all of A.D. Ellis's M/M romance at https://books2read.com/ap/RWrrNx/AD-Ellis

Sign up at http://www.subscribepage.com/ADEllisNewsMMRomance for a FREE male/male romance book.

This is a work of fiction. Names, characters, places, and incidents are either the product of the author's imagination or are used fictitiously. Any resemblance to actual persons living or dead, business establishments, events, or locales is entirely coincidental.

.

AUTHOR NOTE

Please note: Raiden's description and perception of himself are *not* the author's own creation. Rai's character was modeled after some very real people with very real perceptions and life experiences. Rai looks at himself and feels the way he does based on the input from real people who saw themselves and felt the same way. Rai's experiences with his family and life in general are based on real people's similar experiences with their family and life experiences.